"There's a bit of magic dust over The Golden Verses. It is composed of wit and imagination—in rare supply these days. Barbara Miller has a vast reserve of this commodity and sprinkles it liberally over all her writing. Enjoy!"

—Marsha Newman, author, lecturer

"Barbara Miller, with artistic and uncanny insight into human kindness, foibles, and flaws, paints her rustic characters using lively word strokes as they experience common life and intense biblical moments. A transformation must-read."

—Patricia A. Peterson, author, editor, writer

"After reading Barbara Miller's intriguing tale of how six well-placed copies of the Good Book changes the recipients' lives, you'll want to read The Golden Verses again for yourself."

—Janet Peterson, author, editor

D0366385

The Golden Verses

The Golden Verses

BARBARA MILLER

CFI
Springville, Utah

ISBN 13: 978-1-55517-946-0
ISBN 10: 1-55517-946-0

Published by CFI, an imprint of Cedar Fort, Inc., 925 N. Main, Springville, UT, 84663
Distributed by Cedar Fort, Inc., www.cedarfort.com

LIBRARY OF CONGRESS CATALOGING-IN-PUBLICATION DATA

Miller, Barbara, 1939-
    Golden verses / by Barbara Miller.
        p. cm.
    ISBN 1-55517-946-0 (acid-free paper)
    1. Mormons--Fiction. I. Title.

    PS3613.I53247G66 2006
    813'.6--dc22

                                            2006014949

Cover design by Nicole Williams
Cover design © 2006 by Lyle Mortimer
Printed in the United States of America

10 9 8 7 6 5 4 3 2 1

Printed on acid-free paper

To dreams and dreamers, young and old

CHAPTER I

The Old Seller of Books

THE OLD MAN skittered through the open autumn door like a heap of shuffling leaves, all crackles at the joints and rustling in the folds of his clothes. Charles expected to see a trail of dried maple foliage on the dusty floor behind his visitor. The door to his bookshop closed softly, as if pulled by the slight October breeze just outside, while the tinkling brass bell announced his uncommon caller.

"May I help you?" Charles asked the old man.

"To the contrary point, young man," the stranger replied.

Charles was thirty-eight years old and did not consider himself young. The ragged looking fellow continued. "To the most contrary point. I may help you. I am in possession of six extraordinary books, which I must sell tonight. They will be cheap, but in the end you will wish you had paid far more for them."

Charles began to speculate silently the old man's idea of cheap. Two cents apiece was cheap to Charles, because the bookshop—though he loved it, pampered it, and mortgaged it—did not support him well. He inquired after the contents of the books.

The cloud of fine grains and air settled around the ancient fellow during the moment of silence that followed Charles's question. A faint aroma of the autumn just outside clung to the man's heels, mingled with the gentle spiciness of fallen apples. The old man's face crinkled in a thousand places. He was smiling.

"They are holy books, Charles—Bibles, special Bibles, with passages printed in gold ink. Not all of them, mind you, just certain ones. When you read them, why, they just come to life for you. They stir the silence in your soul. They make the stories come to life!"

Charles was taken aback. "Gold ink *passages?* I know about gold leaf edges but not about gold ink passages. Won't the printing wear away?"

Charles considered gold to be soft, delicate, almost like a whisper. Gold ink seemed a stretch beyond his tired imagination. He was trying to picture passages of gold without asking to see them. Everyone knows that if you look at a salesman's product, if you heft it and feel it, then you've just about bought it. He shook his head to convince himself, as much as the old man, that he did not wish to see the so-called gold-ink Bibles. Hoping to derail the seller, he asked quickly, "How did you know my name is Charles?"

"Last question answered first. Your name is on the sign just outside above that door. No one but the owner of such a small establishment would be here this late, and on a Friday night, especially. First question answered last. Does the handprint of God wear away from the mountaintops, or do the stars diminish from so much shining? No, Charles, and this ink does not wear away."

The old man rushed across the floor to one of the display shelves. At his side bounced a leather bag, bulging clumsily on four sides. It obviously held a box.

"You have good books here, Charles. No trash. Hugo, Dostoyevsky, Shakespeare—although I don't know about this Fitzgerald person. No matter. These Bibles that I will sell you far outstrip any of the others in impact. You'll see."

Charles marveled at the man's brash manner. He looked like a walking heap of mold, in more than slight need of a good bath. Yet he conducted himself as if he were offering diamonds for the price of glass. Charles could not help himself; his curiosity was piqued.

"Well, then. How much do you want for them?"

"The cost for each is one dollar and twenty cents. Six times that cost is not too much, and you should be able to bear that. You may sell them at whatever price you deem reasonable."

Charles calculated quickly. "Yes, well, the total then is seven dollars and twenty cents. I don't know. This has been a slow week." He was hesitant, knowing that his till held very little money.

"Let's not quibble, Charles. I know you have that much and that there are people here in your little town who desperately need these books. Buy them!"

Charles was suddenly a bit annoyed with the attitude of this seller of books. He had never seen this man before in his life. Already he had placed himself on a first-name basis and was practically ordering Charles to part with the paltry few dollars he had in the till.

"Look now," Charles said, raising his voice only slightly, for he was generally soft-spoken. "Nearly everyone here already has a Bible; some folks own two at the moment. I know that for a fact. No one has come in asking for a Bible in months."

The old man was now growing a bit testy. "Well, then, advertise them for *Christmas* gifts, why don't you? Use your imagination, man!"

Charles had never encountered such a brazen salesman—old and almost brittle in appearance, dusty around the tattered edges, and acting as though he himself ran the bookshop. Despite his irritation, Charles suddenly felt drawn to respond positively. "Well, the gold ink passages *might* make a nice selling feature. Let me check my till."

The register drawer popped out with a familiar ping! It was jerked back by a strong spring, and the loose change flipped, landing heads up, two out of three. Charles carefully counted the bills and coins. A chill passed over him. There was exactly seven dollars and twenty cents, to the penny!

The big hand on the schoolhouse clock behind him inched, trembled, and twitched its way toward twelve, and the trusty timekeeper chimed the eighteenth hour. Its ticking filled the tiny shop, sounding very much like his own heartbeat, reminding Charles that he would be late meeting his wife, Greta, for the yearly Fall Fest at the community center. It also reminded him that if he spent the last money in the till on Bibles, Greta might become very upset. The bookseller smiled benevolently, every other one of his crooked old teeth gleaming gold. He swung the leather bag from his hip and dumped its contents on the counter. A wooden box tumbled out and wobbled on one corner before thumping to a rest next to Charles's hand.

"Obey your compassionate instincts, Charles. Buy them."

Charles felt the old man's stare fixed on him, like the watery gaze of a desperate beggar. A bit unsettled, Charles hesitated and then said, "It appears you have a very nice touch at guessing a register's contents. Or perhaps you are just lucky." Then, thinking of Greta, he continued. "Whatever the case, I really cannot buy your Bibles today. Perhaps if you pass this way again next year or in six months. . ." He slammed the drawer shut.

The old man's face fell suddenly and sagged like a balloon out of breath. The wrinkles draped themselves over his fragile bones, looking as if they might decompose with his next sigh. "But, Charles," he implored, "you don't understand. If I don't sell these Bibles tonight, I am without means entirely. Nowhere to go, no substance to support my life, meager as it already is. Please believe me. You will not only be helping out those who buy, but you will also be giving a poor pauper a last chance to make something of his time."

Charles was again wary but oddly touched. "What? You mean you would lose your job if these aren't sold? Surely your employer couldn't be so cruel."

"It is just that as soon as the books are sold, more good can come of them. Their messages are wasted lying in the confines of this old box. My employer is interested in the spreading of the word."

He turned his face from Charles and blew his nose loudly into a grimy, gray handkerchief. Charles could have sworn he saw tiny dust mites fly from inside the man's loose sleeves and the hairs in his ears flutter with the huge nose-blowing effort.

Charles may have been a man of little means, but a true hard-luck story would persuade him to part with any worldly possession to alleviate another's suffering. The frayed and pitiful spectacle standing before him melted his already-thin armor of defense, and his inner heart was softened. He would just have to deal with Greta later.

"Well, all right then. I suppose I will just have to buy your Bibles and be done with it!"

He hurriedly popped the drawer open once more and pulled out the seven dollars and twenty cents. "Do you mind if I don't count it again?" He asked. "I really have to be going!"

The seller of books turned and looked in the direction of the door behind him. He shivered and appeared to be overcome by trepidation and a need for haste. The old man was also eager to leave. "Good thinking, Charles. We had both better get going."

He quickly stuffed the empty leather pouch into his pocket and took the money. "I reiterate, my friend. You will not be sorry you made this purchase, no matter what your wife says and no matter how things look on the surface. Good day now. Perhaps I'll pass this way another time."

The brass bell jingled, and the door swung behind the old man, sucked closed by the chill autumn wind. Charles watched him walk out and knew he would quickly be swallowed by the darkness beyond his shop lights. Suddenly his eye was drawn to a barely perceptible change in the atmosphere behind the old bookseller. It was like a shadow in the air—smoky and thinly transparent, almost alive, as it seemed to follow inches from him. The sight was so unusual, so spectral, that Charles ran to the door and burst through it, calling out loud, "Sir! Sir!"

As he looked into the street, he saw the old man rounding the corner, moving fast, and the shade hanging behind him but keeping pace. He was anxious for the old man and curious at the same time. He ran from the door to the end of the street and looked in the direction of the bookseller's departure. He saw nothing, no one. The tattered bookseller had disappeared and with him, the apparition.

When Charles returned to his shop, the telephone was jingling on the wall behind the counter. He answered, breathless. It was Greta, barking on the other end of the line.

"Why are you still at the store, Charles? We're already late for the welcome. It's a good thing I didn't have to serve on that committee this year, but everyone will be wondering where I am for the bake-off. You'll just have to spruce up as best you can and walk over by yourself! And for heaven's sake, try not to overbid on some piece of junk at the silent auction. I'll see you there!"

Charles had no time to apologize—and he certainly would have—or to explain his tardiness, and he still clung to the receiver after Greta had clanged the other end down. He realized the unsteady condition of his nerves when he slowly released his heavy grip on the receiver, uncurling the fingers one at a time. Greta he was accustomed to, so her abrupt manner did not bother him much anymore. It was the filmy, gray phantom he had seen, floating in a hurry after the bookseller, that had rattled him. He was absolutely sure he had seen it, for his eyes rarely deceived him. He felt a queer sort of rush now, quickly threw the box of Bibles under the counter, and left the shop.

As he walked along the darkened street, Charles puzzled over the past few minutes more and more. The old man's remark about not minding what his wife might think struck him as peculiar. Did the bookseller know by instinct what kind of woman Greta was? Was it so obvious that Charles, being mild mannered, would have married a shrew? Another thing bewildered him. The old man had seemed half lame when he entered the bookstore, yet as he left and Charles watched him scurry away, he showed no sign of age or a limp. What about the money? How could a complete stranger have guessed the exact amount Charles had in the till? Even Charles had not known.

Charles rounded the corner where he had lost sight of the merchant and the shadow, and he was at once enveloped by a dark, forbidding awareness. He shivered while passing through the circles of light from the yellow street globes, for he felt his shadow gliding like a separate being, now behind him, now in front. The hollow quiet of the night suggested to him that he was alone, and the streets were void of everyday faces.

Uneasiness enfolded him, and Charles soon increased his pace, forcing himself not to look back over his shoulder, uncertain of what he might see in the shadows behind.

CHAPTER 2

Antiques

SATURDAY'S WIND was warmer than Friday's, and it blew a light freshness across the little town. Charles had crawled into bed the previous night surrounded by a foreboding spirit, awakened twice by unexplainable shivers.

"It comes from walking around without a sweater in this weather. You are so absent minded, poor dear!" Greta had an answer for all of life's "preturbances." That's what she called them, anyway—"preturbances." Charles always resisted the urge to tell her that *preturbance* was not really even a word. No matter. Now, looking through the upstairs windowpanes and bathed in the sharp light of this autumn morning, last night's cloud had, in small part, recessed. He thought he might like to putter around in his garage a bit before getting down to the serious business of Greta's kitchen bench.

Saturday mornings were generally given over to Greta's projects because the opening of the shop was left to the school-girl assistant, Dory. As he pulled on his old woolen slacks, he remembered he had left the till empty. Dory would need some change. Second thoughts reminded him that business had been slow lately, so the chance she would see any buyers this morning was small. Still, at breakfast he announced to Greta that he would be going to the shop for a short while, but he would be right back to paint that kitchen bench for her.

It was too bad about Greta, though. She seemed never to get much permanent joy, or real satisfaction, out of life. He knew that, while she said having the bench painted would complete the look of the kitchen, sooner or later it would take something else to placate her. Charles, on the other hand, was completely absorbed and at peace in his bookshop. It was small, to be sure; some people called it cozy. It was unassuming, but his regulars called it homey. Its best feature was being filled with books. Charles imagined heaven itself as one gigantic library, boasting shelves and shelves of worn volumes, the best works man had to offer, and the finest scripture and books of philosophy the world had ever known. Perhaps there would be a section for a celestial accumulation devoted to the writings of angels and other-worldly peoples.

"See to it that Dory doesn't sit around reading and wasting the hours while she's there on our time," Greta complained. "I've been thinking that maybe we ought to let her go. Then I could handle your off times myself. We would save wages that way, and with Christmas coming, we could use the extra."

Charles's reverie and pleasant flights of speculation were interrupted by Greta's sharp voice and crass suggestion. He snapped back to her world immediately. Managing to counter her gently, he said, "Greta, what would Dory do then for earnings? She needs the work. No, I can't let her go, not now. We'll find another way to save if we need to."

He turned away as the vision of the box of Bibles played in his head. He had bought them last night, sight unseen, and spent every last cent in the till to do it.

Best not tell Greta about those just yet. "I'll be back soon," he called, hurrying out the door.

Charles and Dory arrived at the bookshop at the same time. As usual, she was quiet and went about straightening and rearranging, dusting with a somber but pleasant expression on her face. She was one of those nearly invisible people, slight and pale, but Charles found her dependable and thoughtful with the customers. He stepped behind the counter and brought out the box of Bibles. Even the box itself reminded him of the old man, damp looking and musty smelling, speckled with the gray dust of mold around the edges. It had the look of half a century or more of use. As he opened it, a tiny silver moth escaped, leaving its powdery companion lying on the cover of one of the Bibles. The books were stacked in two piles, three volumes deep. He picked one up and studied it, dismayed at the shabby appearance. It was frayed, ill smelling, loosely bound, and worst of all, seemed to have the word *sucker* engraved on the cover. "Well, obviously, these books cannot be sold. We'll just have to give them away," he said aloud.

"What's that, Mr. C.?" Dory thought he was talking to her.

"Oh, nothing, Dory. It just looks as though I was taken in last night. I bought these Bibles from a sad-looking old man, who seemed to really need the money, and they look like something he salvaged from the dump. He put on a good show, though. I was stupid to have bought them sight unseen."

"Well, Mr. C., how could you know he was gonna stiff you?" Dory fingered one of the Bibles, leafing through the pages. "Sometimes there's nice pictures in a Bible." She stopped her page turning and looked at one of the passages. "Look here, Mr. C. This printing is all in gold. My aunt has a Bible where Jesus' words are in red, but I never saw one with gold before. Maybe that's what makes them special."

Charles recalled the old man's words. They make the

messages come to life. "That may be so, Dory, but who would pay for such beat-up-looking books?"

"We could call them antiques," she offered.

Charles did not often consider the use of gimmicks to sell books, but he saw the possibility here. "Dory, you may have struck on something! I'll tell you what. You make us a nice little sign, sort of old fashioned, to advertise these Bibles, and we'll give it a try. Besides, I'll pay you a commission of ten percent of each sale, if you like, and we'll see about getting rid of them."

Dory set to work on the sign, smiling with excitement at the offer made by her employer. As Charles pulled a fragmented feather duster from beneath the counter, the moth that had liberated itself from the weathered box settled in the ribs of a lamp shade in a far corner of the shop and resumed sleeping. Its companion was brushed off the Bible and sent fluttering in several pieces as Charles resumed dusting his hand-me-down purchases. As he examined the Bibles once more, he reassured himself that the antique idea was a good one. The books certainly looked old enough, and who knows, maybe somewhere in his town there actually *were* people who needed them. Maybe the old man was right, after all.

CHAPTER 3

The Business of Burying

OWN THE STREET two blocks and around the corner, a
man dressed in a navy blue pea jacket and wool pants
swept the entry to his establishment. Leaves had nested rather
firmly in the niches of the doorway, and he shuffled them out
with great vigor and a very stiff corn-straw broom. He was
in his middle years, forty to be exact, slightly paunchy, and a
smoker of long black cigars. "See-gars," he called them. His
business was preparing the departed for their final rest and
sending them to their great reward, which he believed to
be nothing, for he saw no benefit in an afterlife. The gold
and black letters scrolled upon his doorway proclaimed most
sedately "Atwood's Mortuary, Theodore Atwood, Undertaker." He had wanted to add the word *extraordinaire*, but his
banker advised against it, saying that it was too pompous. His
slogan read, *Rest for the Departed, Comfort for the Living.* Theodore himself was not sedate, nor was he very comforting. He
was, however, the only undertaker in town, so people had to

go with him or drive twenty miles to Clairesville, over east, as they say.

The week had been slow, so Theodore busied himself repairing leaky faucets, because the drip-drip spooked his part-time assistant, and replacing the dangling plaster in the main chapel. The plaster bothered him—he did not want to lose a client over a falling piece of ceiling! Theodore knew that business would pick up after autumn because winter was a natural time for old people to croak from living so long and young people to cash in as a result of accidents.

Theo hardly ever used the word *death* or any of its proper derivatives. Instead, he boasted the finest collection of euphemisms concerning that inevitable end this side of the Mississippi. He was careful not to use the hard-hearted ones in front of actual cash-money clients whose loved ones had recently passed on, but he filled the air of his back rooms with colorful double-speak.

"Look here," he would say to his assistant, or maybe just to himself when he was alone. "Old Mrs. Stone here lived a long life. It was about time she bought the farm and checked out. She conked out doing what she liked best—playing bridge— so what's the big deal? When I bite the dust, I want to be at home, chewing on a big, fat stogie. I'm gonna lay down my last card there, and when I do, it'll be the ace of spades. Ha, ha! Get it? Spades? Yep. My crossing the bar will happen only after I've been to one and had my winding-up swig."

Theo's attitude may have seemed a harsh way to view life and death to gentler souls, but Theodore was a hardened individual and always had been. He did not get into the mortuary business because of his comforting nature. His old man had started the business and had shown him the ropes before he reached the age of ten.

Today Theo bid good morning to those who passed by, nodding his head vigorously and asking after each person's health. He was, at least, friendly. Some folks were put off by this friendliness. "I always get the feeling he's measuring me up or checking my skin color," one would say. "I'll never shake his hand, you know. There's no telling where it's been."

When he had the chance, he liked to argue the impossibility of an afterlife with staunch believers. "No, my friend," he would say, "once you are planted (another favorite euphemism), that's the end of it. Some say you come back as a dog or cat or something, but why would you want to? And why would you want to go on somewhere else, flying around in cold, dark space forever with no see-gars? Ever see a painting of an angel smoking see-gars? For that matter, ever see a picture of angels doing anything but blowing trumpets and hovering around some kid's bed? Naw, the stiffs don't bother me because I know they're just a rag, a bone, and a hank of hair. Sit up? Sure, I've seen 'em do that, but it's just gas, you know. Ever see a chicken run around with its head chopped off? Saved up energy, that's what it is. Now, wouldn't that be a sight—old man Anderson running down the street in a sheet, headless as Ichabod's horseman? No sir. The only things that ever come up again once they're turned under are flowers and noxious weeds."

Clarence Anderson was the oldest living human in a five-county radius, and according to his spinster daughters, he was within inches of death at any given hour. They had changed funeral plans for him so many times it was funny to everyone except them. They took the business of burying "dead seriously," so to speak. Originally Miss Hoskins, the organist at First Presbyterian, was going to play all the music, but she died three years ago, and the daughters did not care for the young upstart who played there now. His music was too jazzy, they complained, and they tried to get him transferred to Clairesville, but the board had signed him up for five years so they were stuck with him. Instead, the ever-practical sisters now planned on using high-quality phonograph records of old time Protestant favorites for the music.

At any rate, Theodore was fairly comfortable with his position in the community, and the slow season never bothered him. *Ah, yes,* he thought, *Old Man Winter will soon cuddle up with a few elderly citizens, wrap his cold arms around them, and ever so gently slip inside their bones.* Then Theodore would be busy at his craft and might even be able to afford that new rolltop desk he had been thinking of. All those pigeon holes!

Across town, however, a surprise awaited Mr. Atwood. Almost overnight, a sign was erected, announcements were posted, and it was noised about quickly that a second undertaker had set up shop. The very morning after the new man opened his doors to everlasting rest, Clarence Anderson turned in his union card of life and went toes up. Theodore loved that expression. Toes up, so apropos, so germane. Theo was knocked for a complete loop when Clarence's younger daughter, Ardis, rang him on the telephone and withdrew any previous arrangements to have Atwood's handle the funeral.

"It's not like we ever signed papers, Theo," she reminded him coldly. "And he who *was* the only undertaker in town had ought to reevaluate the overblown fees he has been charging through the years. Adele and I have always considered ourselves to be forerunners in the community, and so, to welcome this new man, we are sending Daddy over there. He brings in an organist from Clairesville who plays for a pittance of that fee you charge to wind up your cranky old Victrola, he has fresh flowers, and most of all, he is a *true believer!* He says Daddy already has a home in heaven and is most likely reunited with Mama and our other dear ones who went before us. Mind you, it's nothing personal, Theo, but we feel better about Daddy being taken care of by a true believer. Not that there's anything *wrong* with being a heretic. . ."

Click!

Ardis regarded Theo's abrupt slamming of the receiver as complete understanding and gently replaced her receiver on its shiny, black hook. She turned to her sister, Adele, who was shaking her head and bursting at the facial seams, no longer trying to suppress a great deal of laughter. "Ardis," she finally managed to say, "you always did have a way with words."

"Well, a heretic *is* a heretic, no matter how you try to dress him up as a free thinker. Theo will be all right. There are plenty of non-believers in town, and they will keep right on dying and their apostate loved ones will pay through the nose to send them on a short trip to the cemetery, with no hope of rising out of that box Theo puts them in."

Somehow the sisters had not gotten over the notion that Theo's atheistic ideas would automatically override their own faith. Adele stood and smiled benevolently at her younger sibling. "You make perfect sense, dear. Let's have some tea and thank our lucky stars that this new man came at just the right time."

Theo was not thanking his lucky stars, since he also did not believe in luck, and he was not thanking the Anderson sisters, either. He had counted on Clarence's viewing to draw a large crowd from all the surrounding communities. It was not often people would get to see a person of Clarence's age in one of Theo's gilded caskets. It would have made for a terrific promotional opportunity.

He chewed ferociously on one of his long, tightly wound see-gars and sat back in a massive horsehair love seat, burning his brain for some kind of counterattack. Fresh flowers, eh? Live, sedate organist, eh? What else was it? Oh, yes! His competitor was a believer! Flowers he might manage, and maybe he could lure the organist over since he was so cheap, but the believing feature was another matter. That would have to be mulled over, schemed, and carefully orchestrated. Perhaps he had been wrong in allowing himself the luxury of free speech in such a provincial little berg. Maybe a month of Sundays in Reverend Gillette's drafty church would turn his reputation around, or at least hint that Theo was reconsidering the resurrection issue. Theo shivered at the thought of sitting through the reverend's diatribes on doing good and whatever else it was a preacher came up with to burden his congregation for the coming week.

Theo's fuming continued. Then he thrust himself out of

the love seat and into the street. A walk would do him good, maybe give him a better idea, a slogan or something to avoid the actual churchgoing thing. It was certainly a beautiful morning for a walk, so clear and cloudless, bathed in a liquid kind of sunlight.

As he neared Charles's bookshop, his thoughts were interrupted by the tinkling of the brass bells above the entry. He looked up but saw no one enter or leave. *Strange*, he thought, *must have been the wind.* He stopped and stared into the shop window. Dory was just finishing the little arrangement of Bibles and placing the sign behind them. Theo's eye was drawn to the words, "Antique Bibles—Special Purchase— *Like the Ones Your Grandmother Used to Read.*"

"Well, I'll be dipped!" he said aloud. "If that ain't one of my answers right there!"

He wheeled into the store, and yanking the cigar out of his mouth, he challenged Dory in a loud voice. "See them Bibles you just put out? How much for one?"

Dory cast a questioning glance at Charles. He nodded her way, hinting that she should set a price. "Er, well, I think . . ."

The ever-impatient Theo fairly bellowed at her. "I'll pay two dollars and not a penny more! Pick me out a real old-looking one."

Dory was twitching all over from the offer but calmly walked to the window and picked up the first Bible her hand touched. "That will be two dollars, sir," she said and held out her shaking fingers.

He grasped the book with an iron hand and held it up for examination. Dory ceased breathing for a moment. "Perfect!" Theo exclaimed, slapping two dollar bills into her hand and then jerking open the door. The bell jingled almost merrily as he left.

Charles stood open mouthed at such an immediate turn of events. Already he had seen an eighty-cent profit. Why, if each of the Bibles went for two dollars he would make. . . he stopped himself. To imagine that anyone else would pay that much, well, it made him giddy. Best forget such projections and just hope that the other five would go soon.

Theo marched straight back to the mortuary, put the "antique Bible" on the desk in the entryway, and snatched off the dusty and pale silk roses. He rescued a copy of *The Mortician's Review and Monthly Catalog* from the trash basket in his office and began to flip through the pages. He leafed quickly through the advertisements featuring caskets, vaults, and flower arrangements to the back where he had seen religious paraphernalia. He found crosses of metal and icons and paintings. There were prints of *Our Lord in the Garden*, *Our Lord on the Cross*, and *Our Lord Knocking at the Door*. He could have identified more easily with one of *Our Lord Going Bankrupt* but decided to settle for the most benign image, the door setting.

I might be able to live with that one, he thought. He would send away for it and also order a small wooden cross, carved with a dogwood theme. There was never any question that the actual crucifix was too harsh an image for this community. The Anderson sisters would certainly never put up with it, since they viewed themselves as gentle women. Hah! *About as gentle as vipers in your underpants*, he thought. Theo retired that evening, growling and spitting tobacco shreds from the mangled cigar, cursing all the good folks in the community who might share the spinsters' rustic views.

Theo smarted from thoughts of the new mortician. It galled him to think that some young whippersnapper had gotten the upper hand on him the first time around. It bothered him worse that he would have to compromise his good name among the heathen just to get on with the business of burying.

CHAPTER 4

Something There Is Which Does Not Like a Bible

CHARLES CONGRATULATED DORY on her first sale of the day. As it happened, it was the only business done with the Bibles that day. Other than that, she sold only a few pamphlets and a copy of Poe's works. A woman and two children did come in and peruse the children's section, but Dory had seen her often and knew she would not be buying. From their appearance, Dory could see they were needy, and the books never failed to excite them. The mother smiled as she listened to the children's small efforts at reading from old favorites, and she did not embarrass them by correcting slight errors. They stayed for nearly an hour as usual, and neither the boy nor the girl pressed their mother to buy anything. Needy children understand from the cradle that asking is not getting, so they do not ask.

Dory closed up at five on Saturdays. She had been alone all afternoon and now decided it would do no harm if she stayed an extra few minutes and look through one of the old

Bibles. It was the pictures that intrigued her, and she liked the crinkling feeling of the ageless pages as she turned them. She was in no particular rush to go home anyway. Her old maid Aunt Ginny was always at culture club until six on Saturday, so she would not be missed.

She locked the door and turned off all the lights except the lamp in the back corner of the shop, where she might sit unnoticed and undisturbed. As she reached up to switch the bulb on, her hand brushed against the sleeping moth. The insect twitched and fluttered wildly inside the shade until, like a pale, silver ghost, it swooped away and disappeared into a space between Alcott and Anderson. Dory was startled and jumped out of the chair, her skin popped all over with goose-bumps. She felt that odd sort of buzz in her ears that people sometimes get when confronted by winged or fuzzy insects. After a moment, she spoke into thin air. "Silly old moth!"

She sat down once more and opened the worn, shabby book. She did wonder how much Charles had paid for these Bibles and why he had not looked through them before he bought. At first, as she flipped through it, she was only vaguely aware of the sound of her own regular breathing and the ticking of the schoolhouse clock across the room. Then she noticed a disturbing scritch-scratch coming from the direction of the store window. *The moth must have flown to the glass,* she thought, *and it is trying to get out.* Soon, however, the scratching became louder and its rhythm more insistent. *Look up,* it seemed to say. *Come to the window, come away from your reading.* Dory did look up.

Outside the window, she saw it. It seemed to be clinging to the glass, a flattened and misty gray shape. Not a moth at all, not a bird or a person, but somehow scratching the glass with impossibly long and slender twig fingers. Dory's heart jumped to her throat, and she cringed behind the chair. Anything she had ever read from Dickens or Edgar Allen Poe paled in her heightened excitement. Whatever this thing was, it moved as if it were alive. Her desperate imagination groped for some sane meaning. Perhaps it was only a large piece of newsprint, caught and held fast against the glass by a strong wind. The busy fingers were nothing more than bits of stiff string. Maybe her eyes were playing tricks in the evening dusk. She remained absolutely immobile. Almost against her own will, she pressed her eyelids lightly closed and retreated farther into the corner.

At length, she heard a key slip into the lock of the door, turning slowly and deliberately. She huddled deep into the dark reaches of the room, trembling and cold. The door swung open silently, and a gust of wind brushed through the shop. The lights snapped on immediately, and she saw Greta standing by the counter, searching for the bank bag. Greta peered around the room and detected Dory crouched in the corner. She was startled that the girl was still there and further startled to see that she was hiding.

"What is the meaning of this?" she demanded. "Why are you still here?"

Dory emerged shyly from her refuge and tried to speak. She was all mumbles and excuses and still shaken from the apparition at the window.

"You were reading what? You saw what? Speak plain, girl. I can't make heads or tails of anything you're saying!"

Greta towered over the young woman. Dory held out the old Bible with a quaking hand, explaining that it was something Charles had bought the night before. She then excused herself quickly and stumbled through the door toward home. Greta looked at the Bible with unbelieving eyes. "What is *this*? Where did this old thing come from? Charles just bought *this*?"

She retrieved the bank bag, stuffed it into her large handbag, and headed for the door. Somehow, she failed to notice the cloudy, gray puff of mist that muffled the brass bells as she closed the door.

CHAPTER 5

An Imperfect Man

PERHAPS SOME SMALL space in this narrative should be allotted to Charles before the story unfolds further. To be exact, Charles was not quite forty years old. He was not quite five feet eleven inches tall and weighed not quite one hundred and sixty pounds. He was no longer as trim as he used to be, "not so skinny," as Greta would say, but he still was healthy and hardly ever knew a sick day. His eyesight, from having perused thousands of books, was a bit dimmer than in his youth, but his insight had grown quite a bit. Those eyes conveyed compassion, which drew some folks to confide in him, while others tried to take advantage of him. Greta became the most unabashed user of this gentle man. As he grew more benevolent, she increased in cantankerousness, thinking of him as a weakling and losing respect for her husband.

Escape from her sharp tongue sent Charles to the bookshop for hours on end, fussing over it, lingering in its quiet warmth. He hung on to certain precious volumes there, reading them over and over. He reviewed new books, recommending only the best books to his shoppers. It was no surprise that the Bibles fell into Charles's domain. He would have sold them for cost and felt lucky to get that. The seller of books must have known that Charles would never think to cheat any buyer and that, through him, the books would fall into the right hands.

Charles was not without faults. He was forgetful, he dawdled, and he often stared into the empty sky when he should have been mowing grass or shoveling snow. It was only that the great expanse above him was so fascinating, so splendid and broad, so full of free air and color. He often forgot to mend her chipped porcelain cups or take out the trash on cold winter nights. He sometimes neglected his duties in writing messages down, and she would miss important meetings. He certainly was not a perfect man. Still, the seller of books must have guessed that Charles would be a compassionate conduit through which the Bibles would pass. The seller of books must have known a great many things about Charles. He must have known the secrets of other townspeople as well. Charles, in his turn, would try to guess the secret of the old man and the shabby, wondrously decorated Bibles.

CHAPTER 6

Mary Magdalene

U NHAPPINESS SEEMS TO follow certain folks around, to wait on a cold doorstep for the approach of chosen individuals. Sadness curls up under these folk's sheets to people their dreams with troubled visions. Spotting these unhappy ones is not always easy, however. Although some do wear the sad face of martyrdom and make careers of complaining and harping, others, such as Lottie Mariah, slap on more makeup or change hair color to disguise the melancholy in their lives.

Lottie was forty-two years old and single. Her body was beginning to thicken around the middle, and her feet were killing her most of the time. She did hair in her front parlor and had a steady flow of female customers. She was good at a man's haircut too, but the women all sent their husbands to Clyde Whipple's barbershop where, they said, a man had a spittoon to use and other men to chew with. Though it was never mentioned, the vibrant undercurrent carried the message that Lottie's parlor was off-limits to any man who wanted to stay even semihappily married. Status quo was the rule, and everyone knew what Lottie's status was. She, of course, knew better than all of them put together and accepted the fact. She was the child of a failed marriage; her mother ran off one day with a pock-marked auctioneer and left her to grow up in the house of her alcoholic father and a worrisome grandmother. By the time she was fifteen, Lottie had learned the hard lessons of life in a town the size of a postage stamp. Here, everyone's ear was to the ground, and a person could not sneeze at three in the afternoon but what the news of it showed up in the evening green sheet. Lottie looked for love and acceptance in dance halls and other wrong places, so before long she had built a dandy little reputation for herself. She left home at seventeen and went "over to Clairesville," as they say, to learn the hairdressing trade. Now, that is honorable work, everyone said, and more or less dismissed her. When Lottie was thirty-two, her father succumbed to a liver ailment, and Lottie returned to inherit the house he had miraculously managed to pay off. "At least he never let his drinking interfere with his work," some wag kindly noted at his funeral.

While away, Lottie had learned survival and even put some money aside for a nest egg, so she decided to try her luck at setting up her own beauty parlor. She had few customers at first, but word was soon out that she set a fine perm and knew all the latest styles. Now, six years and several suitors later, she was still unmarried—why buy the cow when you can get the milk for free?—still tainted by her parents' failures and still dogged by her own desperate attempts to find happiness. She had finally accepted this as her lot in life but managed to hide her misery with remarkable success. She may have been suffering inside, but to the world, she showed a happy face, even if she had to paint it on every morning.

Lottie was approached one day in this fine, golden autumn by two of the ladies in the Naomi Circle. Very proper women they were too, in their brown crepe dresses accented by starched lace at the throat and the wrists. Actually, she had been approached several times about joining this group that met on Wednesday evenings to make things for the needy. This Wednesday they would be crocheting doilies for some underprivileged church in some unpronounceable place, her visitors announced. Lottie knew that the prime reason she was invited was to see if they might save her soul. This was not mentioned in the invitation, but Lottie realized it anyway. She was not sure she was ready to have her soul saved just yet, so she politely put them off. She felt like saying that the underprivileged needed doilies about as much as a polar bear needed boxing gloves, but she refrained. She did, after all, do these ladies' hair on a regular basis.

Still, when Wednesday evening rolled around and she found herself alone as usual, the prospect of sitting with other females began to assume a warmer glow. Perhaps there would be at least one of them she could talk to, maybe someone new in town who had not known her family and would not want to redeem her by the end of the week. She had halfway decided to stroll over to the church, but this anemic resolve was abandoned after she sat down and got a load off her feet. With only one lamp lit, her house soon became dark around her as the sun sunk below the horizon. Her eyes swept across the room where, as a child, she had witnessed so many arguments between her parents. The memories were unpleasant, and she often was seized with an overwhelming desire to escape from this place. Yet, here she was, leading a common life, alone and drawn by convenience to a home she once had gladly left. That fringed lamp shade still reminded her of the "floozy mother" (she had given her mother that name herself) who abandoned her years before.

So many other things called up the memories, the old gloom. She did well enough hiding that sadness when people were around, but by herself it was sometimes impossible to mask. She was too tired to light the cold-gas fireplace on this melancholy autumn night. Pulling a wool afghan around her body, Lottie curled up further and buried herself in the chair. She soon dozed off to sleep and, after a fifty-minute nap, dragged wearily to bed. Oh well, she was not very good at crocheting anyway, and that poor church would do well enough without her clumsy efforts.

The next morning, Thursday morning, was the time that she gifted herself to get away from her work, the house, the fading India carpet beneath the swiveling chair in her parlor. This day was beautiful in general and was wonderful in particular because she could enjoy the sweet, warm October sunshine. Last week's rain had ceased, a few leaves still colored the trees, and she felt blithely free. She stopped by the drugstore to replenish her supply of women's magazines for the clientele. She knew some of them would never spend a dime on *those kinds* of magazines, but since "there was nothing else to read" in her beauty shop, her customers read them cover to cover while sitting under the dryer. Lottie was amused. She reviewed the pious invitation from the church ladies.

"They're the worst!" she thought, and a cunningly wicked plan nestled in her mind. She paid for the magazines and sauntered smugly past Charles's bookshop. However, the display in the window caught her attention, and she marched directly into the shop. Charles had not often sold books to her, but he knew who she was. As we said, this was a small town and "a sneeze at three o'clock" was heard everywhere. She came straight to the point. "I see you have old Bibles for sale. How much are they?"

"Miss Mariah," Charles greeted her with a nod. "Good morning. Well, they were something of a special purchase, you see, and that's why they are so worn looking. I'm asking a dollar twenty, but only because they contain a very special feature. You see, some of the passages. . ."

"Yeah, yeah," she interrupted him. "Whatever. I'll take one. It'll be worth it just to see the old bags squirm."

"Excuse me?" Charles answered.

"Never mind. Pick me out your nicest one."

She took it from him and, without so much as a look at the flyleaf, plunked it into her mesh shopping bag, paid him, and left, chuckling to herself. That afternoon, when Adele Anderson showed up at Lottie's for her weekly do, the only reading material to be found on the end table was Charles's antique Bible. Lottie watched slyly as Adele's eyes scanned the room in vain for the familiar magazines. As she sat under the dryer, Adele pulled out notepad and pencil and began making a grocery list, then doodling on the borders, and finally going through her purse and discarding scraps of paper and balls of dull pink lint.

While Adele's hair was still drying, Lottie took out her newest magazine and began to leaf through it, displaying great interest and amusement in the articles and pictures. She raised her eyebrows and shook her head, reacting in elaborate pantomimes to the juicy gossip she pretended to read. Adele cleared her throat and spoke loudly from beneath the hot air machine. "Do you have something I could browse through while I dry?"

Lottie nodded her head and, as deftly as a cat cornering its mouse, handed Adele the Bible. "Just picked it up today!" she bellowed. "Thought you'd like that better than this!" Her blood-red fingernail pointed to the dashing, mustachioed film star featured on the magazine's glossy cover.

Adele smiled weakly and absently flipped the pages of the Bible to Revelations knowing that in her few minutes remaining under the dryer, she could pass over verses that the Lord never expected her to understand and skim through doctrine she was never required to discuss in depth. Revelations, as a book, was safe for the layperson, because you could read it, not comprehend it, and still get in your scripture time.

Lottie peered into Adele's eyes for the slightest hint of dissatisfaction. She was not disappointed, for she detected a filmy dulling of the iris as Adele settled in to the seventh seal and the star whose name is Wormwood. Neither of the women was aware of the passages highlighted in gold, so when Adele

closed the book, its words had made no difference. The significance of the unique verses would wait for another time.

CHAPTER 7

Three Down and Three to Go

NEARLY A WEEK had gone by when Charles concluded that he had been swindled by the crafty old bookseller. He took a brief and embarrassing inventory of the Bibles. One, which he had brought home, was lying in a box with other throwaways intended for the indigent. Greta had tossed it there during a verbal storm. She had called on her flair for the phonetic, and this time her words raced each other across the room, sinking into him like a bee's stinger.

"I can't believe," she began, "that you spent our *last* dollar on such ragged, dog-eared, beat-up old books. I cannot comprehend how you allowed—no, how you *invited*—a complete stranger to bamboozle you into buying, *sight unseen,* even one, let alone a *half dozen,* cheap, seedy looking Bibles! I'll bet they're not even translated correctly. You are," she berated, "a sucker of the first water. We ought to just have 'cheat me' tattooed across your forehead and be done with it!"

First of all, thought Charles in silence, *it wasn't exactly our last dollar.* Greta herself managed to take care of that at the silent auction. Second, the Word was the Word, even if it was housed in shabby clothing, and the antique approach seemed to be working. Third, if he had been duped, it was at least in the name of kindness. Or was it just to get rid of a pesky salesman? Charles was busy asking himself this question when Greta changed her tactic.

"Charles, dear. You really must leave buying to me. Now, the next time some slick itinerant comes into the shop, you tell him you have to consult with your purchasing agent and ask him for a business card. Just say we'll get back to him."

He hated this patronizing tone even more than the nagging criticisms she most often employed. He had hardly thought of the seller of books as slick. To have been gulled by a bonified slicker might have excused his blunder, but to have been taken by a walking dust ball caused Charles the innermost chagrin.

He went on with his inventory. Besides the one at home, there was the one bought by Theo Atwood, most likely sitting on a table at the mortuary. The third was snatched up by Miss Mariah. Charles had a hard time believing she had suddenly caught fire on religion, so he correctly assumed that it was for her clientele. *Nice gesture*, he thought innocently. The other three rested mutely in the window of his shop, absorbing the afternoon sun like old, weathered cats. He could see them from where he stood.

About three o'clock, the brass bells tinkled above the door, signaling Dory's arrival. She seemed unusually cheery. "Mr. C., I have another idea for selling the old Bibles. How's this? We have those children's encyclopedias you've wanted to sell for a long time. You talked about reducing the price of them anyway, so why not go ahead with that and offer a Bible with each set for a dollar extra?"

Charles nodded his head as she spoke, liking the idea immediately. "Yes, yes! That's great, Dory. We'll do it. Make up a new display, and I'll take care of business."

Fifteen minutes after the display was set up, the mother of the two children came in, the quiet one who seemed to be absorbed in the world of her offspring, gliding silently through the shop on thin-soled pumps. The children were not with her, something singular. Her excursion through the aisles stopped abruptly at the encyclopedia display. She fingered each volume gingerly, seeming to absorb knowledge through her very fingertips. Then she lifted one of the Bibles and peered through its pages. Doubtless, the gold ink struck her, for she stood transfixed, eyes a glaze, apparently reading some mystic enchantment in the passages. Dory approached her, and when she opened her mouth to offer assistance, the woman smiled and made a hasty exit, mumbling a wilted "thank you" on her way out. Suddenly, she poked her head back through the doorway and asked quickly, "How much for those books again?"

Dory read the special pricing exactly as she had written it, sounding somewhat stiff. "The full set is offered at ten dollars, and you receive the antique Bible at one dollar extra."

Her name was Nancy Rutledge. When she left the shop and hurried along the street, she rubbed her fingertips together, still able to feel the books in the empty air. The orange-colored covers of the encyclopedias were hard and pebbled, leaving a rich and smart sensation on her hands. They were etched with clever drawings to illustrate the stories found inside, and to Nancy, they represented the greatest of gifts she might ever give her children. The Bible summoned an entirely different response. It was soft, pliable, and smelled of ancient paper; its pages fluttered softly, like leaves of transparent tissue. To touch it was the same as stroking the cheek of a wise old aunt, warm in years, soft and delicate but strong all the same. She had seen something in the Bible that startled her, and seeing, it was as though her eyes were opened for the first time in her life.

She estimated over and over the cost of the books against her ability to pay. Though they were significantly marked down, the price seemed too high. Nancy walked quickly now toward her home. She had spent too much time in the bookshop and hurried to get to the three-room clapboard house where her children waited. Her husband would be back soon and expecting supper to be ready.

Even in a rush, she was good at cooking suppers from nothing much and would have to do the same today. An onion in the water pot made for a pungent beginning, and she had learned to throw whatever else she could glean from her garden or cupboard in for the makings of soup or stew. Tonight it would have to be soup, since there were no more usable bones or sinews from the butcher this week.

Her children were obedient. They had stayed inside the little house while she was gone. "Mommy's going to look for work, little ones," she explained earlier. "I want you to take care of each other while I'm out. I won't be long, all right? You take care of each other."

Nodding, they watched her go. They wondered why their mother needed more work, since it seemed she had enough to do already in their own small house. They had visited the homes of their school friends and knew that other mothers did not have to work as hard as she did. They knew also that they did not live the same way as their friends. Coal was placed a few small lumps at a time and burned judiciously in a potbellied stove, instead of being shoveled into a basement furnace and allowed to distribute heat throughout the house. They also still employed the drafty outhouse in the narrow plot of dirt they called a backyard. Instead of water flowing into an indoor sink, Nancy pumped water from a spigot outside the back door.

Worse than any of these misfortunes, however, was the murky cloud and foul mood under which they all lived when their father was at home. The children were still young, but every year they grew closer and closer to the realization that they were from the "wrong side of town" and that their father was set apart from other fathers. They had not yet arrived at the knowledge that they and their mother were the objects of condescending pity. These things did not hurt them yet.

CHAPTER 8

The Ladies' Meeting

NANCY RUTLEDGE AND her brood were often the objects of concern at the Naomi Circle meetings in the church parlor. Mr. Rutledge's character, disagreeable as it was, allowed for all the righteous indignation the women could muster, which was voluminous. The Rutledge name would come up, almost as part of the agenda, and the discussion would launch itself, something like a poltergeist, and fly around the room from one tongue to another.

"I wouldn't stay a day with a man like that! Say, Mary, I love that stitch!"

"His drinking will be the end of the whole family. I've seen it happen before. My sister over to Clairesville could tell us all about that. Where'd you find that shell pattern anyway?"

"I sent away for it last month out of a catalog. Well, as far as I can see, a man like that doesn't care a fig for his family. I'm surprised they're not already on the dole."

"Cora, I just love those little rosettes. That pink is perfect. And, if you ask me, no good will come of him taking that job with the railroad. First thing you know, he'll be on the train and out of here. Leave her flat, that's what he'll do, and she'll be abandoned to raise those children alone."

"Ha! She should be that lucky! Although, good men *are* scarce as hen's teeth nowadays. She'll wind up in the poor house for sure. Pass me those scissors, would you, Lillie?"

So on and so forth went the ladies' meeting. Only the week after the new undertaker moved in did the subject vary.

"I heard Theodore was positively florid when the sisters changed their funeral plans and sent their daddy to the new man!"

"My dear, Theo is florid most of the time, don't you think?"

General titters went around the room.

"Well, I say it serves him right! He practically throws his hedonism in your face every time he walks past you on the street. Poor Reverend Gillette has suffered the man's diatribes for years."

"He's a saint, for certain."

"The reverend? To be sure!" It sounded as if she had said, "Tubby sher." "And Theo will fry on the other side." This comment was followed by an indignant, all-knowing sniff and a comprehensive, assenting "harumph" from all but one of the group.

"Tish, tish, Cora," Adele said. "We mustn't form opinions so harshly. Remember the scripture, 'Judge not that ye be not judged.'"

Cora raised her chin to justify her own statement. Her sniff was a little too loud. "Well, surely you don't think that Theo and the reverend will wind up in the same pew over there, do you?" A slight halt and chilly pause fell upon the group.

"I'm sure I couldn't say who is going where. It's only that I heard Theo is showing signs of conversion. We must not give up on anyone, no matter how reprobate he may seem." The ladies lowered their permed heads and made mental notes to clam up around the gentle sisters from then on.

"You see, when we did take Daddy to the new man, Mr. Angell, he kindly advised us that Theo is also part of the human race, making him our brother. He suggested that we treat Theo with a little more kindness. After all, look at his background and consider our advantages. Even at that, none of us are perfect."

She hesitated a moment. "Or is it, none of us *is* perfect?"

CHAPTER 9

Gifts

THE FOLLOWING MORNING the Misses Andersons happened into Charles's bookshop and upon Nancy Rutledge. Nancy had returned to have another look at the encyclopedias and the Bible. She was speaking earnestly to Charles.

"I was wondering if I could pay just a little at a time and have these bought by Christmas. My babies would love something like this, and they know how to read pretty good already."

Charles was silently calculating how much she might pay per week to get the set by Christmas. It would not be too much, but still he was aware of her pinched circumstances. "I can hold them for you at a dollar a week until then," he said, discreetly.

"A dollar a week? Does that add up to eleven dollars by Christmas?" She posed her question timidly.

"Yes, ma'am, it does. We could also gift wrap them if you like."

"Hmm. Gift wrap? That would be real special, wouldn't it? What would wrapping cost?"

"Oh, that would be free. It's a service we have at Christmas." Charles did not consider this to be an on-the-spot fabrication, since he had often entertained the notion of gift wrap for those who made large purchases. This would amount to a large purchase for her, and all things being relative, Charles felt justified in his offer.

Nancy could not commit immediately and pondered a moment before answering. "If you could just hold a set for another few days, I'll need to see about getting a little job on the side so I can surprise my family."

Ardis and Adele eavesdropped shamelessly behind one of the tall displays and recalled the speeches made at the Naomi Circle meetings by the incensed women. When Nancy left the shop and was well out of sight, the sisters primly approached Charles.

"Charles, we couldn't help but overhear your conversation with Mrs. Rutledge. We know a little about her situation, and we've seen her children. They are little darlings and bright too, though they tend to hang back because of their circumstances. Well, you know, what we mean to say is, you needn't hold the books and wait for her to pay for them; we would like to purchase them for those children and have them delivered. You know, from an anonymous donor. It would be an early Christmas perhaps, from Santa's elves or something like that."

Charles was flabbergasted. Such magnanimity, right out of the blue! This type of transaction had never occurred in his little shop. Oh yes, every so often he would get grannies buying favorite books for grandchildren, or frantic husbands looking for last-minute gifts, but not out and out charity. He thought it was a fine idea.

"A fine idea!" he spouted, a hair too loudly. "How very nice of you. I can have Dory deliver them, and she can truthfully say she doesn't know who the elves are."

Ardis withdrew her checkbook and filled in the blanks on check number 901, signing it with her distinctive flair. "Would you include a gift wrap on that, please? "

"It will be done today, Miss Anderson. Thank you both, very much!"

The sisters exited the bookshop sporting the inner glow of those who have performed a charitable act. No one would call that which enveloped them pride. They did not in the least imagine what an unhappy dilemma it would create for Nancy Rutledge. To be fair, no one could have known, because no matter how awful he already looked to the gentry, Jack Rutledge was much worse in private.

By noon the day became rainy, the sky was toneless, and the streets absorbed the gray drizzle. Iridescent rainbows swam in puddles beneath parked automobiles. Autumn still clung to most of the oaks, but the other trees were dropping leaves daily. Jutting from black trunks, the branches reached knotted fingers up to the leaden sky. The weather had cleared a bit by the time Dory arrived at work, but the clouds still offered very little breach for the sun. She said she would not mind the walk across town to deliver the books. It would mean a nice break from dusting and rearranging displays. Perhaps a small sprinkling of the glow the old sisters felt had infiltrated Dory too, since it was her display that had prompted the sale.

The girl's bundle was less large than cumbersome, but she did not mind. To walk to Nancy Rutledge's house was not so far. The town was minuscule after all. The distance did not amount to much, but the house itself was decidedly removed. In getting there, one passed around or through the cemetery that lay behind the Methodist church. The expanding plot was filled with Andersons and Wallaces and others of staunch church membership. Massive oaks shaded the graves of those buried longest, but one imagined that the roots might play havoc with their comfort. What peaceful rest could be had when one's coffin was invaded and tilted by giant, cloying rhizomes? Here and there a newly upended headstone played host to whitened grass roots and colonies of crawling insects, all clinging to the underside of the granite marker.

Dory slipped around the iron-clad burial ground rather than pass through it. Suddenly captured by an uneasy, chilly feeling, she clutched the parcel of gift-wrapped books close to her chest. She dared not look behind, for she experienced the same buzzing in her ears that had preceded the appearance of the gray shape on the shop window. Her steps quickened, the thumping of her heart became heavier, and her breathing was shallow. She spoke aloud to herself and to the blustering wind. "Silly Dory! You've walked past here a thousand times. There's nothing to be afraid of!"

Yet she was afraid. Hurrying, she came at last to Nancy's door. The house stared at her through two small shaded windows flanking the warped door. It apologized for such a sad appearance in the voice of the mournful draft whistling under the saggy roof and through tiers of ivy from the sloping eaves. The yard was bare except for a few pickets at the head of a stone walk. Rain and snow and beating sun had worn away any paint that might have covered the old wood. The house stood bleak and ragged now. Dory raised her hand and knocked timidly.

The door opened slowly and standing before her was Jack Rutledge himself. He was a red-haired man; his face was grizzled by a multicolored growth of three days. He wore dirty clothes and leaned his body toward the open doorway, swaying slightly. Detecting the stale odor of smoke and strong drink, Dory reeled back a step or two.

"What do you want?" Jack's deep voice was blurred, but she understood him well. Dory quaked and then gathered her nerves and wits.

"I'm from the bookshop on Main Street. I brought a special package for your wife and children."

Jack's eyes squinched tightly, and his mouth curled into an ugly, gnarled root, running across his jaw. He bellowed into the house.

"Nancy, get out here! What is this? Have you gone spending what we ain't got again? What the hell do you need with *books?*"

Nancy came timidly to the door. She recognized Dory and was immediately ashamed. "I don't know, I'm sure. I never bought anything at the bookshop."

"Oh, it's a gift," said Dory, gaining a little more courage. "Someone wants you to have these for your children. I'm to say it's an early Christmas present from Santa's elves."

"You mean *charity?*" Jack roared again.

"Why, no sir. They just thought. . ."

"They just thought what? That I can't do for my own family? Well, they thought wrong! If I want my family to have books or whatever that tripe is from the store, I will damn well buy the stuff myself! I don't need no sob sister dropping off donations to the poor little Rutledge clan. Take your stuff to some other down-and-outers!"

He slammed the door straight in her face. A queer mixture of anger and humiliation shook Dory from hair root to toenail, and she ran nearly the whole way back to the shop. Run she well should have too, for though she did not see it, at her heels hovered the ominous gray shape that had chased the seller of books and rattled itself against the bookshop window. Only the reemerging rays of sun through cloud sent the misty being scurrying away from her. She closed the shop door behind her and breathlessly related the whole story to Charles.

He reprimanded himself harshly. "It should have been me delivering. I ought to have known he might be there. We will just hang onto these books then, until she comes to pick them up or he sleeps it off and repents of his bad temper."

That night, still in a dark mood, Jack Rutledge divested the sugar bowl of its few coins and stormed from his house. As hours passed, the family waited for the dreaded footstep that would bring his rage back, but it did not come. Nancy and the children were on the verge of retiring when a knock

sounded at the door. A man from the railroad station stood
on the dingy doorstep, holding a battered felt hat in his hands.
Nancy recognized it as Jack's.

"I'm real sorry, ma'am." He stuttered and was uncomfortable. Nancy did not invite him in but stepped a few inches
outside the door.

"What is it?" she asked, puzzled.

"Like I said, I'm sorry to be the one to give you this news.
But your husband, Jack Rutledge, fell between two cars on
the B&O freight as it was pulling out. There was nothing
anybody could do to save him. He is dead."

"Oh, Lord," she said, and it was not so much an exclama-
tion of sorrow as a cry of relief.

CHAPTER 10

Everything Counts

WILLIAM HICKEN, A banker, *the* banker, sat in his semi-tidiness contemplating again. Next to calculating sums, the meditation of profit was his favorite pastime. He was obsessed with numbers.

When William tossed balls of crisp, white paper into a basket, he counted successful shots and recorded them. Tuesday, October 28, twelve of twenty tosses made. What percentage was that? Could he top himself tomorrow? Eight turns of the handle on the sharpener achieved the right point on his pencil. Empty the sharpener once a day. Shoelaces wound through six eyelets, and seven buttons closed the front of his shirt, which cost him three dollars. Five pairs of cuff links for twelve shirts. Ten good ties and seven second choice. Four clocks in the bank, synchronized to the second. One wife, two children, no pets. Imagine counting fleas on a pet? Never-ending.

It happened that from his childhood, William Hicken

was hampered with a mysterious heart ailment. Murmurs and quickened beating at odd times plagued him. When he was a boy he spent much time in a sick bed and thus developed his counting habit. There had been rose buds on the wall-paper in his house, a billion of them, each bearing three leaves, and when little Billy had finished counting the rose buds he could actually see, he calculated their unseen numbers until he nearly went mad. He was shuttled from one doctor to the next, year after year. His parents indulged him to an infinite degree, until he began to think of himself as the focal point of all existence. Had he thought about molecules and atoms, he might have gone entirely bonkers. As it was, the counting finally led him to banking, and he worked his way quickly to the presidency of the bank. He was not loved much in that capacity, but then, he was not much loved in any capacity. His marriage to an out-of-towner came as a shock to nearly everyone.

Today he had chanced to visit Theo at the mortuary, warning him to watch for slow payment from Mrs. Oglethorpe. Her comatose husband was expected, like old man Anderson, to kick the bucket any day now. Their finances would not be the best until the inheritance was worked out.

"You really ought to hit her up for interest," he advised.

Theo still smarted from Ardis Anderson's remark about overcharging and replied, "Thanks for the advice, Bill, but with the new man in town, I got to appear magnanimous to a certain degree."

William Hicken, who ran his fingers over any object at hand, now caressed the table top on which lay Theo's newly acquired antique Bible. "Good heavens, Theo! Where did this come from? It looks like something you disinterred!"

"For all I know, that's how Charles got it. I bought it at his bookstore the other day. I figured if I hauled it out here as the one my grandmother used to read it, it would make for a more churchy impression. You know that new man is all over them with his afterlife blather. Makes me want to puke!"

William leafed through the book carefully, fearing it might fall apart in his hands. The gold printing caught his eye. He did not actually stop to read it but found the warm glow of it fascinating, in a fiscal kind of way.

"How old is this anyway? Is it a real antique?"

"Don't know. All I know is, it better help with the atmosphere. You know, they file in, maybe sit here and read a bit, or even just look at it, maybe they get a feeling I actually believe."

"Wouldn't want to sell it would you?"

"Sorry, no. There were more at the store last time I looked. You a big fan of this mythology yourself?"

"No, but I am interested in a good investment. If this was worth anything at all, I could turn a profit on it. Knowing Charles, I'll bet he let it go for a song. Am I right?"

"Why don't you just go right down there, sing a few tunes, and find out for yourself? I got business to attend to."

"Somebody die? Who died? No news came through the bank."

"I don't guess you'd know him. Name's Jack Rutledge. You wouldn't exactly be running in the same circles. He fell under a moving train—a real mess. Then too, I got a catalog man coming by. Going to show me some of the new mahogany line. Seems he even has oversize I could stock."

William Hicken shivered, suddenly remembering what awful things were stored in Theo's back rooms. He, William, was afraid to die and had calculated how many more days he had left if he were to die, say, when he was seventy years old. As the years passed, he allowed himself more time, more months and more minutes. His heart problem would just have to retreat and grant him more years, more time.

The men separated. Theo went back to the straightening of his mortuary, rearranging the fine grains of dust that had drifted through the cracks and open doors. Some called it dusting. He preferred to call it pushing particles.

Bothering the dollars in his pocket and fingering them one by one, William made his way to the quaint little bookstore.

He knew the dollars and cents of Charles's shop and did not often enter such a place. It was terribly busy in all its quietude, busy with thousands of incarcerated pages, book spines glaring to be counted, subject matters, and shelves. How many titles beginning with A, how many rows of A, B, and C? He saw instantly that there was only one of the antique books in the display. Charles had kept one aside, thinking it might make a nice gift for Dory if it had not sold by Christmas.

Charles saw William approach the shop. Quickly he considered the state of his loan with the bank. Calculations bounded quickly through his brain, and he assured himself he was not behind on any payments. He was relieved then to welcome William. Facing a banker, he generally felt, was like greeting Greta on a bad day.

"Hello, William. What can I do for you today?"

"I'd like to see that antique Bible over there," the banker responded, gesturing with a nod of his head.

Stranger and stranger these times, thought Charles. The old seller of books had told him there were folks in his town who needed these particular Bibles, but he would never have foreseen the banker buying one. For that matter, neither Theo nor Lottie would have come to mind. Not that they would not benefit, of course. The Anderson sisters' charitable act was not surprising, nor the fact that Dory was interested in the books, but these other three had come at him from far left field.

"I was selling it in conjunction with the children's encyclopedias. Would you be interested in buying the set?" Charles ventured.

"Encyclopedias? Heavens no!" William pictured himself beginning at the beginning and memorizing inane and useless facts, coordinating all the information on page 200 of each volume. He simply did not have the time! "Just the Bible, if I might."

"Two dollars then. I bought them from a man who specializes in this type of printing. You see, there are passages printed in gold. . ." Charles began to explain.

"Real gold?" William asked, tilting his head to the side and squinting. He was woefully myopic and too vain to be seen wearing spectacles in public.

"I assume so," answered Charles, stammering slightly. "I was led to believe that."

"Well, they seem old anyway, with or without gold writing in them. Two dollars?" William reached into his pocket and fidgeted two bills away from the wad before withdrawing them. It was another kind of game he played. What were the odds he could distinguish the fives from the tens and the ones? He would chance it this time.

"Tell you what, Charles. I will give you the two bills I take from my pocket, no matter what they are. I like to think I can tell the difference between the big ones and the small ones."

"All bills are the same to me," Charles joked. "That's because small 'ones' are all I ever have in my pockets." He chuckled, not really liking his relative poverty but enjoying his little pun.

William rubbed the bills and turned them over a few times before withdrawing the two that would buy an antique Bible. He pulled out a five and a ten. Charles gasped under his breath.

William studied the denominations, disgruntled. "Well, I'll be swizzled! I thought for sure these were two ones. A deal is a deal though. Here you go, Charles. I never go back on my word."

He handed the amazed Charles the fifteen dollars and took a deep breath. Charles was dumbfounded to the point of silence. William nodded at him and tucked the book under his arm, striding confidently to the door. The brass bells jingled like a thousand cash registers in Charles's ears. Outside, William cursed himself for having forgotten that he was only carrying fives and tens today. On the way home, he tried to remember how many of each remained and added their sums until he hit his front door. Only then would he allow himself the privilege of looking. It was too bad he had never thought of visiting a psychiatrist. The rich fields of his obsessions would have invited years of lobal plowing.

CHAPTER II

The Odd Forms of Charity

JACK RUTLEDGE'S DEATH was not yet causing a general stir that morning, but by law of nature such news was known immediately to two people in town: the bartender and the hairdresser. Ordinary folks guessed this phenomenon occurred through some kind of electric charge in the air or other extrasensory means. The Anderson sisters' hair appointment fell the very morning after Jack stumbled into eternity, and Lottie passed the notice to the ladies in her own colorful style.

"He was what most people called a loser, but you know, Miss Anderson, I just think that he was plain lost. He never had a rudder in life, you know. Nobody ever taught him when he was young that drink was bad, and then when he got older, alcohol already had him by the throat. It's a mean mistress, drink is."

"I feel so bad about his family, though," said Adele.

"Well, I don't!" Lottie declared, dropping sympathy for

the rudderless like a hot curling iron. "That woman will be a thousand times better off without a drunk ruining her life! He spent every dime they ever had on demon rum. I should know. I've seen him put it away and never mind where. It's not for ears such as yours. Well, someone will come along and help her out. What about all those ladies that meet on Wednesday night? Seems like they have a hankering to save somebody every other week. Here's one they can sink their teeth into. Say, I'll even cough up a few bucks to save old Jack's babies. Let me know, will you? There! You're finished. What do you think?"

Adele was twirled around in her chair and handed an oversized mirror so she could get a rear view of her hair. She was satisfied. The purple was toned down from last time and brought out the blue of her eyes. "You look wonderful," Ardis chirped and took her own place in the chair.

When the sisters returned home, the telephone was ringing. Charles was on the other end of the line about the delivery dilemma. Ardis commented that now Mr. Rutledge was gone, there should be no problem with delivering the books to Nancy. Charles was surprised at the news. He instantly began to see how much the books would be appreciated, now that the family breadwinner was gone. Nancy would never be able to buy them under these new circumstances. The Anderson's charity would be even more appreciated. He was caught up short when he heard Ardis say, "Maybe we will talk to Mrs. Rutledge ourselves, just to see what can be done. We could give her the books and say they were from the Naomi Circle. We will see to it after the funeral."

"Funeral?" Greta questioned upon hearing the news. "They don't have two nickels to rub together. How can she even pay for a burial? I can hardly imagine Theo Atwood doing it for nothing."

"You forget the pauper's fund at the church, Greta. That's the sort of thing the money is for," Charles reminded her, setting her thinking in the direction of his overabundant charity.

"Ah, yes. The pauper's fund. Something I no doubt will need after you are gone! Honestly, Charles, the way you give money away, you'd think we were made of gold. I'll bet half the money in that fund is from our pocket!"

"Well, I'm just glad it's there for people who need it. You don't have to worry about yourself, Greta. There will be a nice little nest egg for you when I'm gone."

"Oh, I'll probably go first anyway." She shook her head and went about her business. *You just could never please a person like Greta*, thought Charles, *even if you volunteered to die first yourself.* He was glad she did not pursue the nest egg comment. He often wondered himself how they would manage when he was too old to run the shop. He guessed it was a matter of trusting in providence to guide him later on.

Jack Rutledge was laid out in a plain pine box, but Nancy had no wish to view the body. Theo explained that he had done the best he could, but under the circumstances, the results were less than satisfactory. He advised a closed casket and she agreed. Theo had only managed to secure Jack's arrangements because he was balancing himself on a bar stool at Gilligan's when the news broke. He had showed up at Nancy's just after the railroad man left.

The whole ceremony was to take place at Atwood's, and the Reverend Mr. Gillette would deliver a brief sermon. To Nancy's surprise, a large spray of fresh mums and some roses stood by the coffin in the viewing room. The stiff maroon ribbon running across it read: From the Naomi Circle at First Methodist.

CHAPTER 12

Revelations

THERE WAS A brittleness in the sharp sunlight the morning of Jack's service. The appointed hour crept on tortoise feet for Nancy, since she had awakened before sunrise. The children were cleaned and dressed, and she now took an unaccustomed care with her own appearance. To say that she wore her best dress was to assume she had one that fit the category. It would better describe her semblance to report that she put on her least-worn dress, a faded flower-patterned shirtwaist. In spite of Charles's offer to drive them, Nancy decided that she and the children would walk to the mortuary. The young mother needed time in the fresh air to continue sorting her family's future. She would be alone now, a thing which she had contemplated, yet feared, many times. The relief that washed over her when she learned of Jack's death transformed into feelings of guilt. Now, it was almost as if her shrouded wishes had been granted too quickly. She was not prepared.

The service went well. There were only a few people in attendance, and we can count them all at this time. Reverend Gillette officiated, and Theo Atwood stood solemnly next to Nancy and the two children. The reverend's wife, Lila, was there, along with Charles and Greta. Charles had prevailed upon Greta to come, and she agreed, just to see how the pauper's fund was being spent. Lottie Mariah came, and the Andersons represented the Naomi Circle. A train engineer and long-time drinking crony of Jack's stood to one side. He discreetly tipped his hat to Lottie. An official from the railroad attended, bearing a small amount of compensatory money for the widow, along with a disclaimer freeing the rail company from any further petitions on the part of the widow. Last of all, there was a man who was a complete stranger to Nancy but not unknown to Theo. Intuition perched on his shoulder impishly as he recognized his adversary. The new undertaker had slipped in just before the service began.

Theo grumbled silently when the man signed the little white book, the reverend nodded respectfully, and others in the room stared for a moment. Charles found himself studying the man's features intently. The face was familiar in the most mysterious way. He was sure he had seen it before, not just at Clarence Anderson's funeral but somewhere else. The eyes had a certain look, the jaw line jutted and curved in such a way, the thumbs of the hands swept back when he gestured. Charles burrowed into the corners of his mind, trying to root out the scene of any previous encounter. The man turned and looked Charles squarely in the face, and immediately Charles felt he should avert his gaze. It was rude to stare, he knew, but for a long moment their eyes locked, and the papery, tenacious face of the old bookseller came to Charles's mind.

Suddenly, thin strains of Mendelssohn spun off Theo's ailing Victrola, intruding on Charles's startling revelation and then disappearing as the old man himself had. Lottie fidgeted the whole time Reverend Gillette spoke. Death made her uncomfortable, and the smell of funeral arrangements reminded her of her father's service. She only attended this funeral out of reverence for the underdog, having had experience herself in that arena. She figured Nancy Rutledge would need the support. The reverend spoke in terms of those sheep who wandered confused in the hills and of the Good Shepherd who constantly searched them out. He detailed the care and concern for the lost lamb and the pitfalls awaiting those unwary members of the flock. He mentioned Jack's name only once.

"Jack Rutledge was among the lost of the flock," he said. "In his heart there was, no doubt, a seeking spirit that, had it been given the chance, might have found its way home by some other means. We mourn the unfortunate passing of one of our community. It came too soon for him to fully find redemption here on earth. We know that a forgiving and loving Shepherd awaits him in the hereafter. God rest his soul and watch over his little family and take good care of them."

Lottie almost sniggered out loud at the euphemisms the reverend was tossing around. Jack was no more a sheep than a doorknob. She considered him a wolf, a spoiler, a lousy excuse for a husband and father. She imagined that if anyone was awaiting Jack Rutledge in the hereafter it was somebody carrying a pitchfork and a bottle. Oh, yes, Jack would be perfectly happy with that but disappointed to spend the rest of eternity going around plucking harp strings and doing good.

After the reverend's remarks, the music eventually dragged itself to a strangled sort of close. The Victrola wound down in an odd, uneven way. The modest gathering dispersed, and Charles was mildly astounded to note that three of the patrons were owners of the tattered Bibles. The odds seemed rather strong against this sort of occurrence, and he tucked the memorandum away in his mind. The small group milled about for a few minutes, and then the Andersons caught Nancy just outside the mortuary.

"Mrs. Rutledge, if we may. . . er. . . we would like to invite you and your children to our home for lunch tomorrow. Please say you can come. We would be disappointed if you declined."

Nancy looked at her children across the room. They were childishly pulling chrysanthemum petals from the arrangement at the head of the casket. She had tucked the money from the railroad official into her purse, awaiting a more private moment for counting, and was thinking about that when the ladies approached her.

"Why, Miss Ardis, Miss Adele. That's so kind of you, but I . . ."

"No buts, please. Our home has not seen children at the table since the nieces and nephews grew up. We really want you to come. Is one o'clock all right for you?" they asked, using the refined manner in which ladies extend invitations to those with busy social calendars.

"Yes," answered the astounded Nancy. "One o'clock will be fine. If you'll tell us where you live, we will be there."

After a brief dedication at the cemetery, the small assemblage disbanded, leaving Nancy, the children, Theo, and the sexton. The mortician and sexton waited patiently for the family to leave, since it was not customary to lower the coffin in the presence of loved ones. "Do you mind," she asked Theo, "if we just sit here for a few minutes? It won't be long, and then you can get on with the business."

He answered in his most solicitous tone. "Certainly. We'll be back in about fifteen minutes." Just enough time to light up a big cigar and wash his throat with something tasty. He motioned to the sexton to follow, and they left Nancy there with the boy and girl.

"Now, children," she began, "I don't want you to worry what's to become of us with your daddy gone. Like the reverend said, God is going to watch over us and somehow take care of us."

The boy fidgeted and wound his fingers together nervously. "Mama, I don't think he will. I don't think he wants to take care of killers and such."

"What are you saying? Who is a killer in our family?" Nancy was surprised at this outburst.

"We are!" Her daughter answered in a small, guilt-ridden impulsive voice. "Me and Andy are! We wished it would happen, that Daddy would die and leave us alone!"

"And now it's done!" Andy began to cry uncontrollably. "We did it, Mama! We wished it every time he hit us and pushed you around. It's our fault he's dead. Maybe his ghost will come out and haunt us now!"

Nancy sat back, amazed at the burden her children were carrying. In part it was not unlike her own, and she stared momentarily into the vacancy awaiting Jack's remains. "See that hole?" she said, shivering. "Your daddy is going to be there and covered with dirt for as long as any of us live. He can't ever come out of it. God won't allow it, I know that much. And we didn't put him there, none of us. Truthfully, children, I often wished the same thing myself, that we'd be free of his temper and meanness. The only thing I feel bad about now is that I didn't protect you better from that. In the end, none of us could protect him from himself. He's the one who was drunk that night. He's the one who fell on his own under the train. It wasn't your fault and it wasn't my fault, and our wishes didn't make it so. Don't you *ever* believe that you caused it! No matter what else happens, from now on, we are going to be a lot happier, and we'll always be together. You just count on it!"

Nancy was determined that Jack's influence was at an end, that his memory would not haunt any of them. She raised her eyes to the church tower, tears stinging her lids. "Every time that church bell rings, I want you children to thank God we have each other. Thank him for every new day, even on the rainiest, darkest mornings. We have each other, and that chime will remind us of it. Now, let's go home and make some hot cocoa. Tomorrow we'll have a real fine lunch at the Andersons and forget all this."

Adele and Ardis had their own concerns to address. After

they left the cemetery, the first stop they made was at the bank. It was a matter of inquiring after Nancy's housing arrangements. Then they went directly to the bookshop.

"We wish to take the books to Mrs. Rutledge ourselves," they informed Charles. "We will tell her they are from the Naomi Circle. They may offer the children some diversion from this gloomy circumstance."

Charles retrieved the wrapped bundle from under the counter and watched them shuffle from the store into the sunny day. *Too bad*, he thought, *that Greta does not possess a little more of that spirit*. Then, true to character, he felt sorry for such thoughts and brushed them aside. The sisters stopped off at the grocery, planning and giggling like teens. "We'll bake those children our special red-devil mayonnaise cake!"

When the little family arrived the following day, the sisters apologized that perhaps the soup was too hot or the dining room too chilly. However, to Nancy and the children, the atmosphere was as warm as puppies and as peaceful as church. There were no loud outbursts, no throwing of plates, no accusations, and no drained bottles on the table. The children were most impressed with the food. There were seconds if they liked, followed by that rich, chocolate-mayonnaise cake with marshmallow frosting. Surely their father was not the only one in the family that had died. They must have passed on and been in heaven themselves!

After lunch, the sisters sat their guests in front of the parlor fire and excused themselves for a minute. Nancy and her children had not ceased staring at all the wealth of the place. Knickknacks by the dozen, flower vases full and bulging with asters and mums, lace curtains at the windows, electric lamps, pleated shades, beautifully covered overstuffeds. Carpets of oriental design lay on the hardwood floor; there was an upright piano in the corner, delicate doilies cascaded from chair arms, and books displayed from baseboard to ceiling along one wall. None of them could attach names to some of the items that sat casually in the Anderson everyday existence.

Ardis and Adele returned shortly, carrying the package that Jack had refused. Was it only two days ago? It seemed a lifetime already.

"These are for your family, Mrs. Rutledge. They are from the Naomi Circle at the church. Please accept them."

Nancy was breathless, the children were stunned, and the two women were trembling. "Please. Open them now."

"Could we, Mama?" Andy found his voice first.

"I guess you could, since you're my family, and whatever is in there belongs to you."

Nancy was filled with pleasure as she saw book after book emerge in her children's hands. Instinct told her who the mysterious elves might be, but she kept that to herself. The last book drawn from the box was the ancient Bible. This pleased her immensely for a deeply personal reason.

"What do you say to Miss Adele and Miss Ardis?" Nancy urged a response from her offspring.

"Thank you, kindly, ma'ams. Thank you!"

"You and the children can read for hours now," Ardis smiled. "They do read, I assume."

"Oh, they already know how to read, of course. Not so good maybe, but they do all right."

"I imagine you've spent a lot of time reading to them."

"Actually, they learned at school, and my mother used to read to them before she passed on."

"What are some of your favorites?" Adele put the question to Nancy quite naturally. Nancy squirmed and stammered slightly.

Then the boy spoke in a quiet voice. Being here with the nice lady made him feel safe enough to share the secret that his mother kept.

"Mama can't read."

Adele was mildly shocked. "But we've seen you in the bookshop, looking at many books. I know you spend time there."

Nancy's head lowered, and she responded timidly. "I take the little ones because they do know how to read some things, and we look at the pictures too. It's been a good place for us to go."

Adele blurted out her impulsive resolution. "Then we will teach you how to read ourselves!"

Nancy was speechless. These sisters must surely be angels. *If I could learn to read*, Nancy had often thought, *I could find work.* Life might have been a little easier for the family all along, if she could have helped Jack earn the living. Of course, Jack would never have encouraged her, but fate had taken care of Jack. So much the more reason for her to learn to read. She had at least learned how to make her mark on papers by sketching out her initials, but nothing more. Certainly fate and God were watching over them after all.

CHAPTER 13

The Fantastic Dream

THOUGH THE SUN shone, the funeral day had a decidedly sad quality. Everyone's mood was diminished by the solemn atmosphere in the old cemetery. Only the Andersons' generosity lifted Charles's spirit above the dreariness. Other events of the day had served to puzzle him and cause him to reflect. He was astonished at the recent sale of one of the battered and inexplicably desirable Bibles to the banker. Further, he was surprised that William had not examined the book more closely. Charles put it down to the many eccentricities of the human race.

As evening approached, Charles reminded himself that he had not investigated the Bibles extensively either. He decided that this would be a good time to do it. Greta had retired early, saying the funeral depressed her and gave her a headache. All that money just to bury a man, and a nonchurchgoer at that!

It was now dark, and Charles sat in his favorite horsehair

chair, warming himself under an old afghan. He switched on the floor lamp beside the chair and opened the tattered Bible. Adjusting the thin ear pieces of his reading glasses, Charles settled in to read. His fireplace was fueled sufficiently for the evening, and the house was comfortably quiet.

Deciding to see if the seller of books was right about the gold ink printing, Charles began at the beginning. In the book of Genesis, the story of the Creation was entirely high-lighted in gold. *We'll just see*, he thought, *if this helps bring the story to life.* The familiar words came back to him, and he found himself nearly able to quote the whole story as he read. It was wonderful as he contemplated it. A miracle that God could have created this earth out of the void and man from the dust. Soon Charles became sleepy, pulled the afghan around his shoulders, and fell into a deep slumber.

The first vivid impression Charles received came in a whirlwind of blackness, and he could feel space flying past him. He did not soar but felt as if he hovered in a vortex, and the force of the cosmos reeled around him. Matter rolled together before him; light and dark formed explosively out of the measureless void. He was hurled through dimensions and eons of time, surrounded by iridescence and rushing waters. A cloud of vapor was his conveyance, and endless numbers of stars were his guides.

Charles saw the sun send light throughout the heavens all around, for there was no up nor down. It was a great and glorious sphere of heat and dancing brilliance. He sensed it warming a new world even as it formed. He was trans-ported to the new earth and watched seeds sprout from the rich, black loam in the field. Ferns unfolded their lacy fronds, flowers sprang from dark forest floors, and a mist rose from the heads of fresh running streams.

Charles watched countless beasts cavort through open meadows and great whales leap high out of the surging sea. He saw no other person in all of this, no man to till the soil, so to speak. When the frenetic energy of creation was spent, he felt a deep sleep come over him, and all was quiet until morning.

Whether it was a dream or a flight of implausible fantasy, Charles could not say, but when he awoke, it was with a jolting start. He looked at the room around him, felt the chair and the cover, and then switched off the burning light. Had he been there all night? Apparently so, since the clock was now striking seven. The fire was burned to cold ash, and sunlight peeped through Greta's lace curtains. He could hear her on the second floor above him, charging through the hallway, heading for the stairs. She popped her upper body through the doorway and reprimanded Charles as if he were a child or some doddering old man.

"You know, sleeping all night in that slouched position will cause all sorts of gastric problems, not to mention backaches and leg cramps. What were you doing down here anyway?"

Charles slipped the Bible under the afghan and sat up straight. "I didn't want to disturb you, with your headache and all. I was just reading here and fell asleep."

"Well, chop, chop, Charles! Time to get going!"

To get going was not what Charles had on his mind at the moment. He was still reeling from the spectacular dream he had experienced during the night. To merely say he'd "had a dream" would have been an understatement of boundless proportions. It was impossible he knew, but Charles felt as though he had indeed been there, a part of the creation story. Until Greta entered the room, he was actually feeling a little like Adam. She managed to dispel that illusion rather quickly.

CHAPTER 14

Golden Reading

ADELE AND ARDIS threw themselves into the teaching of Nancy Rutledge immediately. Their fire and enthusiasm were nearly too much for the new widow. The month-long study plan contrived by the gentle but firm elders looked overwhelming, especially in the face of her immediate need for employment. She voiced her concern, trying not to seem ungrateful or unteachable.

Ardis was adamant. "Posh! You are a smart woman, Mrs. Rutledge. You can study at night after the children are in bed. As for work, I will submit your name for consideration at the Naomi Circle, and I have no doubt someone there will need your services."

"Do you mean housecleaning and such? I don't know. I'd be nervous around people's nice things. Do you think they'd trust me picking up their good stuff?"

"Mrs. Rutledge, may I call you Nancy? And please, call me Ardis. Well then, Nancy. No one at our church has anything that cannot be replaced if broken, and I can see by the way you've kept your home," Miss Anderson made a small sweeping gesture of her hand in the cramped room, "that you are careful. I wouldn't worry. Let me see about it."

After the sisters left, Nancy studied the alphabet sheets lying on her table. Here and there she recognized single letters, but combinations of vowels and consonants were a jumble. They danced hieroglyphic jigs on the lines, weaving confused patterns across the pages and mocked her ignorance. The only reason she felt she could continue with this instruction sprang from something she had seen hidden in the pages of the old Bible. When she picked it up that first day in Charles's bookshop, she was immediately attracted to the verses highlighted in buttery gold. She felt bewitched, for as she looked at them, their meaning came to her, clear and exact. Her mind was refreshed as the words literally passed through her, and their significance washed over her like warm water. That night, she too dreamed an amazing dream, one in which she was visited by an angel bearing the most surprising news. She had told no one about the dream and hardly believed it herself. She would return to those and other verses, now that the book was hers.

While Nancy Rutledge and Charles pondered their fantastic dreams and the living reality of them, Theo, Lottie, and William had not yet been charmed by the prospect of scripture reading. Theo continued to display his Bible prominently and even handle it fondly when people were present, solely to give a pious impression. He would affect an ecclesiastical demeanor and cast his eyes heavenward, as if he were contemplating things celestial. The Bible was becoming a significant reinforcement to the new image he wished to convey. He had not changed his thinking about the grim reaper and certainly had no aspirations himself about a better life on the other side. The arrival of the new undertaker had not caused any reflections beyond seeking ways to hang onto his gloomy monopoly. Theo did not feel comfortable around his rival.

The undertaker's oddly tranquil manner was disconcerting, and even his name made Theo ill at ease. What kind of name was T. T. Angell anyway? Probably an invention. Well, he couldn't worry about that right now. The man clearly had established his own image right away. As for Theo, the seegar remained, but his disparaging remarks to believers fell off to inaudible mutterings behind their backs.

Lottie's Bible maintained its place on the table in her parlor. It lay beside the stacks of *Movie Magazine* and *Ladies Review*, sometimes getting lost under the toothy grins of stars on the covers of said periodicals. Lottie's experiment had been the success she had expected, but somehow the inner gloating gave her no satisfaction. To speak frankly, she was in a vacuum, and now that old Jack was gone, her own mortality stared her in the face. What would happen to her between the present and the day she died? How would she go, and who would be there at her own funeral? What was on the other side, if there was another side? Seeing how few people came to say so long to Jack, Lottie had not been shocked—rather, she projected her own final farewell. Would the room be just as empty? Would the few who might have pitied her or been curious send a flowered wreath, pay their respects, move on to have lunch with their friends, and then go look for another hairdresser?

William, the banker, now gave no thought to the fifteen dollars he had spent on the old Bible, though he had berated himself earlier. Instead, he began to send for catalogues and seek out information from antiques people on the value of such books. The publishing date on the inside cover revealed that the book was antiquated beyond belief. It could only have been better if the text were in German and it had carried Guttenberg's signature. That it should have survived this long was an amazement, and William knew he could easily recoup his money, maybe even tenfold. For all its deterioration and obvious handling, he noted that no ownership was ever written on the flyleaf, no notes were scrawled in the margins. Thus there was nothing other than wear to mar its original state, and even that would not render the book less valuable. As William calculated future gains from the sale of such a Bible, he began a playful scheme to lure Theo into trading a new book for the old one that lay on his entrance table. If Theo's Bible was as old as William's, many pretty pennies could be had. Further, while sitting before a blazing fire in his parlor before retiring, William decided to see if Charles had any other such books for sale.

The sixth Bible, which William might have bought if his greed had worked on him quicker, fell to Dory. After the banker had more than doubled Charles's original investment by his arrogant blunder, Charles resolved to reward Dory for the success of her advertising strategy. Charles retrieved the last Bible from the window, where it had lain, gathering sunlight and dust, and presented it to the surprised Dory. She stumbled over her words as she received the book. "Oh, Mr. C., I can't believe it. You could make a lot of money selling this last one. I just know that any day now someone is going to walk through that door and practically beg for your antique Bible. I don't know that I should take it."

"Dory, I'm the boss here, right? You take that Bible and read to your heart's content." Then Charles fell silent and, recalling his dream, said in a serious tone. "Read one of those stories printed in gold ink, and then tell me about it the next time you come in. I'd be interested in hearing your reaction."

Outside, a shadow in the graying twilight took note of the exchange between Charles and Dory. It was the filmy specter once again, hanging motionless in a niche of the old brick library across the street. As the electric lights winked out in windows up and down the avenue, the specter moved ever closer to the bookshop. Soon Charles and Dory would be leaving the little store. Charles would walk with Dory as far as the corner and then turn north toward his home. Dory would walk the five blocks to her aunt's house and drop her schoolbooks onto the hall chair before heading to the warm kitchen. It was her daily routine, and her aunt would greet her in a cheery voice at precisely five-fifteen. Tonight it would not happen that way.

Charles left Dory at the corner and was suddenly struck with a vague recollection. Somewhere in the prolific library stored within his memory a disturbing phrase or paragraph inched its way forward. What was it? Where had he read it? Something to do with herbs or potions of a sort, something about forbidden writings and poison—were there properties in the gold ink, he wondered, that caused his fantastic dream of the Creation?

Charles walked quickly back to the bookstore. What he sought would probably not be among the books on his shelves. He seemed to remember reading it from a shabby volume, not unlike the Bibles he had bought from the grimy old bookseller.

Charles now began questioning the wisdom in encouraging Dory to read from those scriptures. He slipped into the store under the friendly jingle of those timeworn brass bells. Heaven only knew how long they had been suspended over that door. They were there when Charles bought the place, and he had liked them immediately, so they stayed. He turned on one small light in the back, not wanting a late customer to interrupt his search. Chances of anyone showing up at that hour were slim, but Charles was determined to find the source of his troubled thoughts uninterrupted.

He sat at his desk, thumbing through a card file that catalogued every book he had ever had in his store; the file even catalogued every book he'd ever owned. Charles looked under the religion category and found nothing. He scanned the cards containing books on the occult and still found nothing. He did not have a section dedicated to herbs or potions, so he began searching for something under hallucinations and dreams. He found nothing remotely mentioning inks or pages. Perhaps in his collection of novels he would discover the phrases he sought. His search led him nowhere, for he remembered that he had taken all of the novels home and shoved them in a basement room. He would have to find it there, he determined.

Darkness was full upon him as Charles locked up the store and headed home. Alarming thoughts pitched and rolled in his mind as he walked over the sodden leaves and through the gathering October mist. He had no idea what the time was. When he arrived home, Greta was agitated and greeted him coldly.

"I suppose you've been at the store this late. I hope some other so-called-salesman hasn't talked you into buying the bones of Saint John or something! Your supper is in the icebox, and you'll have to eat it cold because I'm off to the Naomi Circle at the church." She threw on her coat and whisked past him still reprimanding him. "What you need, Charles, is a mother not a wife. A mother lets you come and go absent-mindedly and serves your every whim. I can't do that. I have my own life, you know!"

Charles did not even attempt to answer her. His mind, while slightly perturbed by her harangue, was still on the basement room where he had put his novels so long ago. He had not ventured down there once since he'd stored the books away. He mumbled an apology into the air and went straight downstairs as soon as Greta was gone. Charles opened the door to the storage room and searched diligently through every box he saw. The containers held quilts, winter clothing, cookbooks, patterns, yarn, magazines, old curtains, even unopened seed packets, but no novels.

None of his books were there. The room seemed to be dedicated to Greta's storage. Where could his books be? He continued his search throughout the basement and even into the attic, but his efforts yielded nothing. He feared the worst, that Greta had thrown his novels away, that she had wanted the space for herself and figured he had enough books at the store anyway. In the pit of his stomach, he knew this is what had happened, and he felt sick.

CHAPTER 15

The Specter Makes a Move

THE TWO TIMES before that Dory had felt the chilling presence behind her and heard the buzzing in her ears, she had found an escape. In the bookshop, the escape came when Greta blustered her way through the door. On the way from Nancy Rutledge's house, the sun had broken through, dispersing clouds. Now the night was on her, and the specter was at home, following behind her, closer and closer.

Dory sensed peril as she rushed toward home. Her ankles felt tingly, as if someone or something were snatching at them. She felt like she was in a dream, trying to run, but her limbs were heavy and dead, as if they were filled with leaded jelly. Dory clutched her books and uttered a small cry of fear. Suddenly, under the dark bower of maples and elms that grew on her street, her breath seemed wrenched from her lungs. Her arms and legs became limp. She discerned a cold, soundless mist right behind her. Immediately fear compelled these words to tumble from her mouth: "Oh, Lord, if you are there, please help me!"

In an instant, the thing that had overpowered her dissipated. She found herself shaking, huddling next to the pile of books. In her hands she still tightly clenched her schoolbooks and the Bible. As she ran the last two blocks to home, she repeated the saving words over and over. Dory burst through the door and ran directly to the kitchen. Her aunt's cheery hello was quickly swallowed behind deep concern and shock.

"What happened, girl? You're as white as a sheet. And shaking like a leaf! What's wrong?"

It was many moments before Dory regained the strength to speak. "Something followed me, Aunt Ginny. I could feel it behind me, grabbing at me, and then reaching all around me, trying to smother me!"

"Did you see who it was?" her aunt asked, backing away ever so slightly.

"It wasn't a 'who,' Aunt Ginny! It was a 'what,' and I think it's come after me before."

Astounded at this narration, her aunt shook her head and asked, "What did this 'thing' look like? When did it come after you before?"

"It's like a dark cloud—no particular shape, but I feel it! It's cold and scratchy and wet, all at the same time. Oh, Aunt Ginny!" Dory burst into fresh tears and buried her head in her hands. "It was at the window of the bookshop when I was reading one of the antique Bibles. It scratched the glass like twisted branches of a tree and was all flattened out against the window, like two things at once, you know, misty and soft, but brittle at the same time. At first, I thought I was imagining things and it was just some newspaper stuck there by the wind."

Then she jerked her head to the side and remembered the same feeling she had while carrying the Bible to the Rutledge home. "It makes kind of a buzzing in your ears when you first notice it. I know it followed me one other time. It was a rainy day that all of a sudden got sunny. The thing disappeared when the sun came out."

"And this time what made it disappear?"

"Yes!" Dory's eyes widened. "That must have been it! I was saying a prayer. But why does it follow me? Why didn't it follow me from the bookshop that first day? It was getting dark then, too."

Ginny stiffened and laced her fingers together. Leading Dory to the living room sofa, Aunt Ginny asked, "What was different about that first time from the other two times?"

Dory pondered each event in the strange series. "All three times, there was no sun." Aunt Ginny smoothed her apron and brushed a few grains of flour into her rounded palm, choosing her words carefully. "So, this 'thing' likes darkness?"

"Yes, I think so." Dory replayed other scenarios. "I had books with me the last two times. It was encyclopedias and the old Bible on the way from the Rutledges, and tonight it was my schoolbooks and the . . ."

Dory hesitated and a chill passed over her. "The old Bible! When I first noticed the thing, I was starting to read one of the Bibles! I have the last Bible with me right now. Mr. C. gave it to me for a present."

Ginny silently digested this information before speaking. After a minute or so, she said, "So, are you thinking that this 'thing' might possibly be after the Bible instead of you. Is that it, dear? Why don't you show me the one you brought?"

Dory picked up the Bible from where she had dropped it at the front door. "It's one of the old, worn-out ones that the traveling bookseller sold to Mr. C. He thought we'd never sell them, but actually he made money on them, even without selling this one."

Ginny turned the book over in her hands and stared at it. Her face bore a puzzled expression. "Why, this looks as old as the hills! I'm surprised anyone would buy them at all."

"Maybe it's because of the gold printing inside. Maybe

they're worth a lot of money because of that."

"If they were worth a lot of money, why didn't the bookseller sell them himself? I'm sure Charles couldn't have paid him very much for them. Charles is not a rich man."

"No, he's not," said Dory. Her expression twisted with deep intent, and her eyes glistened feverishly. "Tomorrow I'm going to tell him everything, so he can warn the others who have the Bibles."

"You do that, dear. Now, let's get some food into you and see if you can get some rest. You've had quite a scare."

After Dory calmed herself and ate, she crawled under her covers and fell quickly into a deep sleep. The Bible remained in the living room, unopened atop an end table. Ginny turned off the lamp without so much as a glance inside its covers and then went to bed. She made a mental note to call Dr. Isaacson in the morning with questions about hallucinations and brain fever.

Outside the window, a seething, shapeless billow hovered just beyond the glass. It pulsed quietly behind the delicate white curtain, staring eyelessly at the Bible. Across the street, a figure passed, stopping for a few seconds to observe. It was the new undertaker, T. T. Angell, who stood watching. Shortly, the thing at the window slithered away, and T. T. Angell continued his nighttime stroll, smiling ever so slightly.

CHAPTER 16

Treasures

THE POSTMAN, ALBERT Lunnen, was a graying man of sixty-three. He had been the sole carrier of secret love letters, death notices, advertisements, and periodicals on the public square for twenty-five years. He delivered mail to the bookshop, the hardware store, the library, the five and dime, the green grocer, and the bank. He could have done it in his sleep and, indeed, often dreamed of his route.

William Hicken had for years received all of his personal mail at his office, so when Albert delivered brochures and catalogues, it was no exceptional event. Today, however, Albert was struck with the unusual numbers of such items he dropped off at the bank. He counted twelve, to be exact, all dealing with antiquities.

Albert literally dumped the lot of them onto William's desk in his private office. "There you go, Billy," said Albert, glad to be rid of his burden. "That's a truckload of reading you got there. Ought to keep you busy for the whole winter."

William hated the way Albert, the letter carrier, called him by that childish nickname. The fact was that William had been a little boy growing up next door to Albert. It bothered William to no end that, even after going off to college, becoming successful as a banker, and assuming airs uncommon to his family, the postman still called him Billy.

"Yes, I'm sure. Thank you, Mr. Lunnen."

William shut the door after Albert, donned a very thick-lensed pair of glasses, and sat down to scrutinize his new collection. Every morsel of information that he gleaned confirmed his hopes that the Bible was practically priceless. Owning one of them would not be enough for William. He expressly determined now to have Theo's copy—and any others Charles might have sold. If Charles was slow enough to miss this opportunity, William assured himself, then Charles deserved to lose out. William's features hardened with the beginnings of a plot, and his appearance changed.

Some might say that William was a handsome man. He sported rather sharp features, however, that could be screwed up into a hatchet-like visage. His wife had not noticed this peculiarity until after their marriage, and by that time it was too late to repent of having wed a curmudgeon. He dressed impeccably, paced rather than walked, gulped instead of enjoyed, churned instead of considered. His temper was quick, and the narrow force of his ego cut him out of society. He had few friends, a fact that did not bother him in the least. In the matter of Bibles, he was at the far end of Charles's spectrum, which was becoming more spiritual and appreciative by the day.

Charles had discovered for himself the real treasure in the antique scriptures. After much contemplation, Charles decided that if the first dream had not hurt him but actually enhanced his life, it would be safe to try once more. The question of inks had not been answered, but he was sure that he had seen the information in a novel, so it was most likely not factual.

The second narrative Charles chose was the tale of Joseph, the visionary brother sold into Egypt by his jealous siblings. That night in his sleep, Charles was conveyed to ancient Canaan and found himself asleep and dreaming. It was a dream within a dream, yet real and tangible. He dreamed Joseph's dream of the sheaves in the field and awoke to relate it to Joseph's brothers who, in this reverie, were his own brothers. He was cast into the pit, sold for twenty pieces of silver, and then went on to prosper in the house of Potiphar. Charles experienced the whole of it, the deception by Potiphar's wife, the prison, the interpretation of Pharaoh's dreams, and the saving of his family in the time of famine.

It was so real that he could feel the rough garments Joseph wore in prison, smell the pungent spices in Pharaoh's lavish court, and taste the fresh water from Egypt's rivers.

Charles awoke the next morning in a state of euphoria. When Greta saw the exhilarated expression on his face, she declared he must have dipped into the cooking wine. She had not seen him look that rhapsodic since he was a young man. Charles was eager to ask Dory if she had read—and if she had, did she dream as he had? When she came to the shop after school that day, he broached the subject. "Did you get a chance to look into the old Bible last night?"

Dory shuddered at the mention of it. She blurted nervously. "I'm afraid of the book, Mr. C. Something dark followed me on account of it. It almost attacked me last night on my way home. I was wondering if the Bible was supposed to be some kind of magic book or worth a lot of money."

Charles expressed astonishment. "What sort of dark something do you mean? Was it a man?"

Dory shook her head slowly. "No, sir, and you might not believe me, but it's the honest truth. It was like a cold, clammy shape, and dark. I sort of sensed it before, at the window of the shop a few days ago. I thought at first it was my imagination. Then I felt it behind me that day I delivered the books to Nancy Rutledge. It's an evil thing, Mr. C. I think it wants the book."

Charles sat down, his mind reeling. What Dory described was exactly the thing he had seen following the old seller of books the night he bought them. He stared at the floor, engrossed in his own recollection of the enigma that had hovered behind the fleeing merchant. Suddenly, he had verification that he had not been wrong. "It can't be!" he exclaimed.

Dory mistook his meaning. "I know you don't believe me, Mr. C. I really can't expect you to; it's such a far-fetched idea. But I swear it *is* true!"

"Oh, I'm sorry, Dory. Of course I believe you! I've seen the thing myself! I didn't think it was connected with the books, only the old man. It followed him too." The two stared at each other for a long moment, trying to digest the meaning of the riddle. Dory broke the silence.

"Why does it want the Bibles? What can be so special about them? Is it the gold inside?"

"I think," Charles answered slowly, "that it's what the gold printing produces that the darkness wants. Have you read any of it at all?"

"No. Like I said, I'm afraid of it."

"I believe the thing that followed you wants you to be afraid, precisely so you won't read it. Do this for me. Tonight, before you go to bed, read from the book. Read some of the verses that are printed in gold. The old bookseller told me that they make the stories come to life. I know for a fact that what he said is true. There is some reason for us to read those stories, and the shadow must want to keep us from it. Where is your Bible now?"

"It was still on the table in Aunt Ginny's living room when I left this morning."

"Do you think she might have read it today?"

"I don't know. She's not much of a reader. She can't see very well."

"Well, here's what I think. Judging from our experience, the thing can't get at people inside a building or when the sun is shining. I've read in my Bible with no problem at all, and I took it home during the daylight."

"That's got to be right. The first time I saw the thing, it was dark, and the shape was outside the window. The second time, it was a cloudy day, and there was no sunshine. Last night, it was dark."

"Wait a minute! What happened when it came at you? How did you get away?"

"I was so frightened that I started to say a prayer. It was gone just like that!" She snapped her fingers, and tears came to her eyes.

"By the pricking of my thumbs. . ." Charles began, and then his voice trailed away. "Dory, something wicked is already here. I'm sure that as long as you walk home before dark and keep the Bible inside, you're going to be safe. I *hope* that's it! The Anderson sisters took one of them to Nancy Rutledge during the daylight, and I haven't had any reports from them about being frightened by anything. I'll see if I can locate the bookseller who sold me those Bibles. We'll get to the bottom of this."

"What about the others who bought the Bibles?" Dory asked.

"Hmm. The only one I might worry about is Nancy Rutledge. I'll contact her tomorrow. Go on home now. You look like you need a day off."

Charles was now in a quandary. How does one locate the wind or put his hands on a snowflake in summer? Where should he begin in his search for the seller of books? The old man had disappeared around the corner that gusty autumn evening with the speed of schoolboys escaping the classroom. What clues had he left? Only the Bibles, Charles reasoned. He would look at his the moment he returned home.

He had just turned the key to lock the shop when he remembered the wooden box. Of course! He was certain the box was still under the counter where he had discarded it. His heart raced as he reentered the shop. Hoping he could find some clue from the box, he scooped it from the bottom shelf where it lay, carelessly placed and untouched since that night.

Charles nervously examined it, running his fingers over the smooth, worn surface. Almost an antique itself, the box featured a sliding cover, which he removed entirely in order to check the underside. Charles drew in a deep, disappointed breath when he discovered nothing. He examined the box once more, turning it over and over. He saw that there were no nails or pegs holding the sides and bottom of it together. It was fashioned, no doubt, by a premium woodworker. The pieces were joined snugly, dovetailed at precise right angles with the finest work he had ever seen. Though the box was obviously aged, it had not warped nor had it suffered dents and scrapes. It was merely worn from much handling. Beautiful as it was, the container offered no other immediate clue. He would have to study brochures from Bible publishing houses for further leads, Charles decided. He returned the box to its place behind the counter, locked up, and went home.

The unexciting life Dory led made it impossible for her to imagine that the reading of passages in gold ink would cause anything other than a philosophical difference in her routine. To please Charles and to force away her fear of the Bible, however, she chose a section in the New Testament that had always appealed to her. In these ancient pages, the Sermon on the Mount was printed entirely in burnished gold. It glowed warmly from the pages, inviting and exotic.

"Blessed are the poor in spirit;" she read, "for theirs is the kingdom of heaven."

Some words melted before her eyes while certain verses leaped into her mind and stayed. "Blessed are the pure in heart; for they shall see God. . . .

"Let your light so shine before men . . .

"For Thine is the kingdom, and the power, and the glory, forever. . ."

Dory felt comforted that night and fell calmly to sleep. No gray, floating mists disturbed her, and her mind was open

to the messages she had read. Like Charles, she awoke in the
morning completely startled by the reality of her dreams. She
had found herself in a gathering of people listening to a Gali-
lean stranger who stood before them. Dory heard whispers
that he had performed miracles, that he drew unto him the
sick and the afflicted and those who searched for a better way.
Dory felt drawn to his message. She followed the crowd along
the dusty road to the mount where the man spoke to his
disciples, and she stood quietly at the fringe. She heard the
words, "Blessed are. . ." and felt tears slip from her eyes and
run freely down her cheeks.

The sun was warm, but a sweet breeze capered on the
hillside, carrying his words to her ears. They were clear and
direct and spoke of peace and hope. She looked about for
familiar faces in the crowd. There were none, but the presence of this man bound them together. She did not feel like a
stranger, and the place seemed familiar, as if she had grown up
there. The simple woven garment she wore was well known
to her, and the fit perfect. The sandals on her feet were sturdy,
and she felt the imprint of her foot in the leather. Even her
toes nestled comfortably in their own little worn impressions.
Her skin was browned by the ancient sun. In short, she was
actually there, and she *belonged* there, listening to the very
message she had read before falling asleep.

When she awoke at dawn, Dory realized completely the
meaning of the bookseller's words. So Charles had read also
and had dreamed as she had. She wondered what verses he
had lived. Further, she wondered, if they read the same story
that night, would they see one another in a dream?

CHAPTER 17

Nancy Alone

THINGS WERE TENUOUS but calm, and Nancy liked them that way. They were insecure but quiet, and she liked that too. The aloneness after Jack's death did not leave her grieving or desperate, nor did she feel lonely. She felt as if it were the end of a long, hard day, as though she had weathered a wearying storm, and now the storm had ceased. The uncertain ocean she had braved was finally still, and she sensed a refuge on the horizon.

Nancy wondered, though, if it were right to feel this way—such relief, such freedom. She wondered also if the remarkable dream she had experienced a few days earlier had been the result of bad beef stock or, as Scrooge said in a play she once saw, a bit of underdone potato. Never had her dreams been so brilliant and so astonishing. Even as a child, she had not undergone such flights of fancy. She thought of sharing the experience with the Anderson sisters but resolved against it. "They may think I'm a little off and decide not to help me with my reading," Nancy told herself.

In truth, the reading lessons were progressing slowly. The connecting of vowel and consonant puzzled Nancy, and she hoped the sisters would not think her stupid or too thick to learn. She need not have worried. Ardis and Adele were of the opinion that Nancy could do it. It would only take time, time that she was willing to spend.

It happened one night, soon after receiving the Bible, that Nancy decided to look into the Bible and "read" the first passages her finger fell on when she opened it. She read and then slept. Dreaming once again, she found herself an older woman, working beside her husband. An ark was being built, for some purpose known only to her husband. The building of the ark took a long time, but days passed quickly in her dream. Rain would come, her husband proclaimed, and all living things upon the earth would be destroyed, excepting those creatures, man and beast, in the ark. She was reviled by all around her for believing and following her husband and was laughed at by those she had once known as friends.

Her sons and their wives joined them on the ark, and the rains began. At first, the rain fell gently, as the water that wets the field in spring. The moisture was welcomed by all, even those who derided her and her family. Then the water descended in sheets and came in gale force winds. Soon, the lightning and thunder joined forces, and the storms became frightening. By the watery hand of the flood, the ark slowly began to rise, and the only survivors of the deluge were those found in the ark's belly.

The reality of Nancy's dream left her shaken in the morning. Her family had landed safely on Ararat, the dove had been sent away and had not returned, and the waters had abated. However, she awoke trembling from another certainty that had occurred in that nighttime image. She recognized one of her sons' wives as Dory, the young girl from the bookshop. It had startled her at first and then seemed a natural thing. She could see that Dory also recognized her, but neither of them spoke of it. They simply lived the dream through together, and it ended where they had both stopped reading—Genesis 8:22.

CHAPTER 18

Halloween

THEO LOVED HALLOWEEN. It was his favorite day of the year, arriving in a season of rich aromas and burnished afternoons, all aglow with sun filtering through the dying leaves. Dry foliage burning throughout the days gifted the town with drifts of blue smoke, smoke that hung on the streets like the misty beards of wizards. The nights were satiny and crisp at the same time, filled with mellow moonlight and wispy clouds high in the velvety night sky. It was therapeutic in an age that did not yet recognize therapy. Though he would not admit it, Theo needed therapy in the worst way. He often recalled his favorite boyhood Halloween, the thirty-first day of October in his ninth year, a night deep and soft and cabalistic. He had lured two friends into the mortuary parlor, promising them candy such as they had never seen before.

"*Licorice* whips ten feet long! Buckets of homemade fudge and red taffy apples, fresh out of my granny's big kettle and sticky sweet. I got popcorn balls big enough to bowl with. Root beer foaming over the mug. Just come on in with me."

Gulled like country bumpkins at a carnival, the two boys trotted innocently into the valley of the recently deceased. Once they were inside the parlor, Theo locked the big double doors and put out the lights. He had rehearsed his moves so many times that he was able to do them in the dark.

"Hey, Theo! What's goin' on?"

Dickie Parker, younger, scrawnier, and skittish to begin with, yowled loudly into the darkness. The other boy, Frank Brady, said nothing but began to breathe funny. In no time at all, he hyperventilated and swooned to the floor. During those few minutes, Theo's flashlight flicked on, and its steady beam illuminated his face from the chin up. In the murky, black room, his ghoulish head seemed to float to the front and come to rest on the closed lid of a large pine coffin. From within the narrow box came scratching and hideous discordant cries.

"*Frank!*" Dickie was frantic. Frank lay flat out on the India carpet, and Dickie tripped over him.

"He's dead!" Theo whispered and then slowly opened the casket lid. The beam from the flashlight hovered above the lid as it creaked upward, and the unearthly noise became louder. "Whoooooo's there?" Theo's voice dropped two octaves, and his eyes bulged, unseen in the darkness. He felt the eye-popping would add to the haunting effect, even though the boys couldn't see him.

As the lid eased open, Dickie rattled the double doors with all his might. Alas, poor Dickie. His effort went for nothing. His heart was failing him fast. Suddenly, all Hades broke loose as a motley conglomerate of cats launched itself from the casket, screeching and clawing, and running madly around the room.

By this time, Dickie was crying. Theo roared. "You Parkers always was chicken!" Frank had revived but lay completely still, plastered to the floor in fear. When Theo switched the lights on, he peered around the parlor and then laughed until tears rolled down his cheeks.

"Suckers! Bawl babies!" He derided the boys soundly and swept the parlor doors wide open. Dickie and Frank scrambled for the hall and tumbled onto the sidewalk, shuddering with fright and spitting mad. Theo's trick had cost him two friends, but he counted the result as worth it. Who wanted to be friends with a couple of pantywaists anyway?

Now Halloween was upon Theo and his little town once more. Tomorrow the spooks would be out in full costume. The thirty-first was called a holiday, though no businesses shut down, no schools closed, and no funerals were postponed on its account. Theo loved to decorate for the season and was just putting the finishing flourishes on his front porch display, when who should show up at his doorstep but T. T. Angell.

"Your presentation is admirable, Mr. Atwood, thoroughly befitting your favorite day of the year. I wonder, how did you accomplish such intricate carving on the jack-o'-lanterns?"

Theo's eyes narrowed, and he nearly chomped straight through the long black see-gar. "And what's it to you? Don't you have a load of dead people to charter to heaven? Surprises me you have time to shuffle around town looking at pumpkin heads."

"Whether people go to heaven is rather up to their maker. I'm afraid a poor mortician has little to do with that. All I promise them is what I read and believe myself. I don't do it to harm you in any way at all. I'm sorry if you interpret it in that way. No, I was just out taking a stroll and happened to come this way. But, you know, people do seek comfort from a mortician. One such man came to me this morning, a Richard Parker. It seems his father just passed away in the night, and he has some rather unsettling memories of your parlor. I hope you don't take offense, since you obviously have been longtime acquaintances. The funeral will be day after tomorrow. Drop by, if you have time. Well, good day to you. And happy trick or treating."

Theo barely contained himself until T. T. Angell was out of sight. "You smart-lipped, smug, pompous, pious, down-wind bag of hot air! Drop by if you have time! Happy trick or treating!"

Theo fumed and foamed through the house and out the back door. He went to his shed to yank out a long-fingered leaf rake, and then he stomped to the front yard. "So little Dickie Parker's old man cashed in, did he? I hope you don't take offense!" He thrashed the ground with the pointy rake and scattered piles of dry leaves in a frenzy. "Drop by if you have *time!* Thanks to you, Mr. Angell, that's about all I do have now!"

It was not until later in the day that Theo reflected on Mr. Angell's remark about Halloween being his favorite day of the year. How did the stranger know that? An involuntary shiver wrapped itself around Theo's shoulders, and he pulled his pea jacket closer across his chest.

Other shivery things were happening at the bookshop. Dory had revealed to Charles her remarkable dreams. While they spoke, Nancy Rutledge entered the store. She and Dory looked at one another knowingly. Electric currents of realization ran through all three of them, and Charles shuffled the two dreamers to a far corner of the shop. After more sharing between them, Charles proposed the next move.

"Tonight, we must all read the same story."

"Something sweet," said Dory.

"Something calm," added Nancy.

"Let's read the Sermon on the Mount," Dory continued. "Mrs. Rutledge would like that, and I would like to go there again."

"Now, Dory," warned Charles, "I don't think it's a matter of actually going there. It's mysterious enough, just knowing that it *feels* like we're there. And who knows what powers are at work, or why you two saw each other? I agree that the Sermon would be good."

Nancy nodded and determined to have Ardis or Adele

locate it for her in the old Bible. She was not ready to reveal her reading problem to anyone else.

Dory posed the following question. "Do you think that anyone else has read? What about Mr. Atwood? Who else bought the Bibles?"

"Besides Theo, there was Bill Hicken, the banker, and Lottie Mariah. That accounts for all of us. I doubt any of them has read yet."

"Shouldn't they know about the dreams? What about the shadow that followed me and the old man?" Dory suspected that Nancy was unaware of the thing.

Charles turned to Nancy and related the story. Nancy was alarmed and feared for the children. "As far as we can tell, if the book stays inside, you won't have any trouble. Just be sure you keep it in the house," Charles reassured her. This whole new world of reading seemed to pose problems she had never imagined.

"Well, then, tonight it's the Sermon." Charles smiled, hoping to crystallize his own thinking. As Nancy left the shop, he shook her hand, nodded, and said, "See you later. Somewhere."

Mr. T. T. Angell emerged from the library at the very moment Nancy left the bookshop. He watched her hasten toward home, and then he crossed the street and strolled casually past the quaint store, deep in his own reflections.

CHAPTER 19

Lottie and the Undertaker

LOTTIE MARIAH HAD finished placing her scarecrow in the front yard, tilting him just so against the big elm tree. She had painted a face on a paper bag head, one that was not dreadful but rather comical instead. She did not really believe in frightening little children. "Real life is scary enough," she always said. He sat on a paper-stuffed rear end, clothed in an old pair of jeans that had belonged to her father. His shirt was traditional plaid, also revived from a box of Mr. Mariah's cast-offs. The scarecrow smelled of attic, straw, and poster paint. His smile was crooked, and his eyes sparkled with glued-on glitter.

To his left, a jack-o'-lantern grimaced where Lottie's paring knife had slipped. To his right, a black cast-iron cat kept guard, regal and aloof. Lottie would dress up tomorrow night as a queen, and the children would think she was Cinderella's fairy godmother. No matter. They loved coming to her house because she dropped wondrous stuff into their pillowcases. Sometimes it was lipstick samples, sometimes tiny vials of perfume, and always tasty candies. The girls kept everything, and the boys would give the perfume to their mothers. Lipstick was kept for writing outrageous messages on mirrors and such.

As she finished and stepped back to survey her work, Lottie saw Mr. Angell ambling along her sidewalk. She immediately recognized him from Jack's funeral. T. T. Angell was not a bad-looking man, she had thought at the time, but when she considered what he did for a living, social ideas flew from her mind.

"Miss Mariah, I believe." He spoke politely and nodded slightly.

"Mr. Angell, I presume," she said. "How're you doing? Nice day for a walk."

"A very good day. I see everyone is decorating for Halloween. I haven't done a thing yet. Will there be many children out tomorrow night?"

"A truckload, every year. The young ones grow up and have more, and the generations just go on and on. It seems like yesterday I was out trick or treating myself."

"That might be fun for a change." T. T. Angell grinned. His broad smile revealed a gold tooth toward the back of his mouth. Lottie could not venture a guess as to his age. He seemed young one moment, old the next.

"Yeah, well, I'm a little ripe to get away with it myself."

Mr. Angell seemed to be reflecting on important words of wisdom, and Lottie could not tell if he heard her. He tilted his head slightly and said, "Would you possibly have the time to give me a quick haircut? I noticed this morning I'm getting a little ragged around the edges here."

She was caught off guard, but missing only half a beat, she answered, "Sure. Just step into my parlor. . ."

"Said the spider to the fly." Mr. Angell finished the sentence for her, and they both laughed. She slipped the oversized linen towel around his shoulders and secured it at the neck.

As she began to cut the hair, she observed, "Your hair is really fine. I don't think I've ever cut such fine hair in my life. Say, are you thirsty? I could get you a soda from the icebox."

"That would be nice," he answered. As she stepped out of the room, he reached to the end table and picked up the old Bible. When she returned, he was engrossed in its pages.

"This is an exceptional Bible you have here. Do your patrons read it while they wait?"

"Not unless there's nothing else to look at. And they're all church women too." She handed him a bottled cream soda. "I bought it as kind of a little trick on them. Just to see, you know, which kind of reading they prefer. Every one of them picks up the movie mags."

"That's too bad. This one has a lot of printing in some kind of gold ink. I wonder if it's valuable."

"I got it for two bucks. It can't be worth a whole lot more than that."

"You never know. Sometimes Bible stories just come to life when you read them at the right time. If I had a Bible like this, I believe I'd read the gold-printed stories first, just to see if there was any special message in them."

Lottie's snipping continued, and they talked of other things. "I don't often get a chance to cut a man's hair in this town, you know. I'm not exactly in the mainstream of society around here." She talked on, unable to imagine why she was sharing her life with this stranger. "I grew up in this very house, and I guess I've lived kind of a wild life. People don't take to single women who have an unconventional way of seeing things. Oh, yeah, I would have liked a family; you know, nice husband and a couple of kids, but I guess it wasn't in the cards for me. I kind of got off on the wrong foot, and I've been dancing on it ever since. I expect I'll be about as popular as Jack Rutledge was when he croaked. The church ladies will come to my funeral just to see how my hair looks. Lord! It'll probably be awful unless I know when my time's come and have a chance to do it myself! I *am* good with a curling iron and brush, I'll say that much for myself."

T. T. Angell listened quietly, and when she stopped her confessional, he replied tenderly, "You know, Miss Mariah, I think as a rule you sell yourself short. I see in you a real kindness, a real insight and gentle spirit. I think you ought to step back and take another look at yourself. There's more to you than you think."

Lottie finished the haircut in silence, not knowing how to respond. After brushing himself off, the new mortician paid her, adding a nice tip as well. "I appreciate your taking extra time to work me in," he said, smiling.

Lottie laughed easily at his remark. "Yeah, you saw how we had to plow through the crowd to get you in. They're just beating down the door. I suppose your business is slow sometimes too."

"Slow but sure. Very few live on this earth forever."

Lottie followed the undertaker through the front door and resumed her work in the yard. She tried not to stare after him, but it was impossible. There was a quality about him, some indefinable mystery, yet he seemed to be someone she might once have known. For the most part, she had been comfortable in his presence. She only wondered at the kindness of his remarks. Nobody had ever spoken that way to her before.

She was still in a reflective mood when Mrs. William Hicken showed up for her regular appointment. Mrs. Hicken had seen T. T. Angell leave just as she came to the shop. "So, is he a nice fellow, Lottie? He's single, isn't he?" She smiled that hopeful smile so often seen on women whose own lives have lost the promise of romance. Lottie replied, "Yeah, he's a nice guy. A little unusual, though. I've never known anyone like him."

That evening Lottie took the unusual man's advice, picked up the old Bible, and began to read. She began reading in the book of St. John, chapter 8. She was no more familiar with the New Testament than the Old, so beginning at the beginning did not matter to her. What she read was at first startling. It spoke of a woman being taken in sin, yet her counterpart had not been accused. Did this seem fair? What about this law of Moses, saying that such people should be stoned? Wasn't that a pretty severe penalty for something that goes on everywhere? She read through verse 11 and then stopped. The verses were disturbing and comforting at the same time. Were they meant for her, or was it chance that caused her eyes to fall upon them?

That night, in a most irregular dream, she knew the awful fear of punishment, as she stood before accusing scribes and Pharisees. She found herself the center of attention before the temple in Jerusalem. Her robes were disheveled, and her hair was in disarray. Her arms had been bruised by the rough handling of these so-called holy men. They dragged her to a man whom they called Master. She hardly dared look at him, but her gaze was drawn to him. He was quiet and dignified, and most of all, she saw no reproach in his eyes. He radiated kindness and a warm glow in her presence. Something in his countenance gave encouragement in this awful, dark hour. She knew in this dream that she was indeed guilty of the accusations, and she knew that *he* knew it. He turned to those who had condemned her, and in a language Lottie had never heard and yet somehow understood, he said, "He that is without sin among you, let him first cast a stone at her."

Lottie immediately knew the meaning of his words. She stood beside him, watching as those who had charged her with sin left, one by one, ashamed. She felt warm and clean all over, something she had never thought possible. His last words to her carried through to her waking the next morning. He said, "Neither do I condemn thee; go and sin no more."

When she awoke that Halloween morning, Lottie checked her bedclothes for the ancient robes she had worn during the dream. She ran trembling hands along her forearms, searching out bruises. The robes and bruises were gone. She was the same Lottie who had slept in the bed all night. Or was she?

Lottie felt unbelievably fresh and somehow washed. She felt younger, more optimistic about the day ahead. In truth, Lottie had never experienced this feeling of total redemption for herself. Never in her entire life had forgiveness washed over her so completely. That man who had spoken to her and reassured her—she knew that man was Jesus, someone she never thought she would come to know. Now, this wonderful morning, she knew that when he said those words to the woman in Jerusalem, he had spoken to her as well. It was revelation, pure and simple, and she could not deny it.

CHAPTER 20

Goblin Crock and Witch Baloney

SOMETHING WAS WATCHING William Hicken that same night. As Lottie Mariah read in St. John and the other three readers took up the book of Matthew, William Hicken pored over his catalogues, gazettes, brochures, and pamphlets. His Bible lay untouched in a desk drawer. His wife and children were making a big occasion of Halloween, working diligently through the afternoon to decorate the entire front yard. The theme was the same, year in and year out. White-sheet ghosts fluttered from bare tree limbs while tombstones dotted the grass. A wooden marker proclaimed, "Here lies Laddie, the best dog ever." Other markers commemorated other bygone pets. "Pretty Polly Parrot, choked on a carrot," and "Handsome, the Tom Cat—Gone but not forgotten." Witches and goblins popped up from behind bushes and lawn chairs; spiders and skeletons hung from house eaves and bamboo poles. The children were thrilled with the results. They had worked hard to scare the life out of their little friends.

It was now dark. In the dining room, William was buried in mounds of antiques and collectibles information. Only the low grumbling of his stomach reminded him it was supper-time. Where was his supper anyway? He rose from the chair and stretched himself, easing considerable stiffness from his joints. He remembered that his family had been toiling furi-ously at messing up the front lawn and went to the window to see what was happening. The shade at his window was drawn, for the western exposure was often too warm inside the room. He reached for the pull and heard a strange scuffing sound just outside the window. "Drat! I'll bet they're hiding in the bushes again. They'll ruin the hydrangeas yet!" he said aloud, as the shade snapped to the top of the window.

Two things happened next. First, the rattle of the shade startled him. He only half expected the noise. Second, staring into the night in search of his rascal children running away, his eyes met with the shapeless mass that followed the old Bibles. It had now found him and pulsed at the windowpane. He felt the cold of it through the glass and saw it throbbing as though it had breath. He backed away immediately, thinking of his wife and children. Thoughts whirling, he ran to the door. He had never seen anything like it in his life. When he leaped through the front door and onto the porch, his family turned and looked at him as if he were someone else. They hardly ever saw William like this—excited, flustered, and out of control.

"Did you see that?" he shouted. "Are you all right?"

They stared at him so strangely that suddenly he felt like a fool. "Oh, it's something you cooked up, isn't it? You and your stupid Halloween decorations! Well, it can just stop right now! You kids get in here and wash up for supper!" Then he shouted to his wife, who was dumbfounded at his behavior. "And where is supper anyway?" Mrs. Hicken and the two little Hickens peered at the crazy man in their father's body. Then they exchanged tense glances and silently picked up their unused holiday trimmings. Something was wrong with

Daddy; they all knew that. Mrs. Hicken herded the young ones inside and urged them to do quiet things while she made supper.

William paced nervously in front of her. "I don't know how you managed that thing at the window, but I want it taken down right now! It scared the life out of me." Mrs. Hicken intended to protest having done anything to the window but changed her mind as he went on.

"I don't know why you insist on perpetuating this stupid Halloween nonsense with the children anyway—all that goblin crock and witch baloney, and tombstones on the lawn. You ought to just cart the kids on down to the cemetery one night and see how thrilled they are with that!"

William's tirade had originated from fright beyond imagination, but only he knew that. However, to castigate the family was a natural reaction, and everyone knows that. That's just the way it works. If ever there was a time he needed a yellow dog to kick around the block, this was it. William turned on his heel and marched straight into a half-open door. His wife stifled an amused snort, pretending it was a cough.

When William reentered the dining room, he cautiously eyed the offending window. He saw nothing outside except the hydrangea bush, swaying gently in October's dying breath. That night, he dreamed too, but not about anything born of reading in the ancient Bible. His wife heard him moan and saw his eyebrows knit with displeasure, but she did not waken him from his nightmare. *He's probably feeling bad about yelling at us*, she thought, and rolled over to her side, satisfied. *That'll teach him!*

CHAPTER 21

Halloween Parades

HALLOWEEN BEGAN WITH that early tang of leaves burning in grandfathers' backyards. Grandfathers are the only ones who burn leaves at such an hour, for these men are morning fresh, eager to prove they are still alive. Dry maple and walnut, withered elm and apple leaf, all popped and crackled together in smoking pyramid piles. Pungent haze filled the air and hung above backyards all over town as another deceased crop of once-budding, blossoming, and unfurled leaves rose above the very trees that bore them. Grandfathers guarded their smoking monuments and watched the past go up in columns of white vapor.

Children woke expectantly, brim full of excitement. Zealous pirates, princesses, ballerinas, and pint-sized Draculas leaped, full bore, from their beds. They hit the bare floors running and flew shoeless to gulp down breakfast. School parades were already organized, and room by room, little spooks and green-haired monsters would await their turns to drag paper chains to the strains of Grieg. "In the Hall of the Mountain King" summoned images of caves dripping with bats and sticky spider webs and evoked visions of vaulted, crumbling haunts. Ah, it was the highlight of the autumn, the crowning event of the season, and no one would be surprised to see pumpkin heads spit out their own seeds, or cats fly across the moon. It was magic then, even more than it is now.

It was a good sunny day but not hot enough to melt wax lips or vampire teeth. Masks of pressed paper hid the small faces of miniature pirates and brides, and green greasepaint produced many an itchy witch. William Hicken's children were in the thick of it, and he was still disgusted. Parents were invited to watch the parade and pass out orange corn candies to the little beggars. Feeling guilty for having yelled at them the night before, William acquiesced and went to the school at precisely three P.M. As PTA president, Mrs. Hicken was also in the thick of everything, so William stood viewing the pageant alone.

After watching the twelfth little person trip by in a bed sheet, William was ready to flee the school building. Unfortunately, his own children had not yet traipsed past, so he was obligated to bear more. He turned to the man standing nearest. "Halloween makes me wish I'd never had children. I'm up to here with it."

The fellow smiled benevolently. "I know what you mean. Children are a test of our patience. But think what your life would be like if you lost just one. I've seen it happen. It's devastating. We really ought to appreciate them while they're young. In no time at all, they grow up, and poof! They're gone."

William had not asked for a sermon on child respect. He was merely making a complaint. He looked at the man's profile and recognized him as the new undertaker. "Mr. Angell, I believe? I'm William Hicken, with First Bank over in the square."

"Yes, I know."

William reached into his breast pocket and pulled out a small card. "Here's my card, in case you ever need to talk about a loan or anything like that."

"Thank you. I hope I don't ever have to borrow, but you never know."

"Well, in case you ever have to invest then." William ventured further conversation. "We have some nice portfolios you might want to investigate."

"Ah, yes. Investments. We are all interested in investments, aren't we? I suppose you like diversity in your plans?"

"Diversity, yes. It's the foundation of the program. Don't put all your eggs in one basket, as they say."

"I hear antiques do well for some. Of course, they vary, and you have to find the right dealer."

William perked up. "Would you happen to know any reputable dealers?"

"Oh, do you have something to sell or are you interested in acquisitions?"

William was fluttering, although he struggled to control his response. "Well, I did run across a couple of antique Bibles. I'm not quite sure of their value, but I've been checking some literature."

"Bibles? Don't sell them, William. You shouldn't sell them at any price."

"Really? Ordinary Bibles are easily replaced, Mr. Angell, but these look to be worth a lot of money. A *lot* of money."

"Maybe you should read one of them first."

"I'm not much of a zealot as far as religion goes. I think I read some required stuff for my catechism when I was a kid. Since then, my wife takes care of the religion in the family."

"She must get lonesome at her church then. What about your children?"

William was feeling a bit of pressure suddenly. He was relieved to see his little darlings come through the door for review. "There they are right now! Rascals nearly scared the pudding out of me last night. You know, idiotic Halloween trappings."

"Yes, I know what you mean. Things that go bump in the night and hang around outside your window, right?"

Suspicions arose immediately in William's mind. Had his children blabbed all over school about his tirade last night? He turned to Mr. Angell.

"Where did you hear that? Say, I didn't know you had kids at the school here."

Angell smiled and patted his shoulder. "I don't. I just came to see the parade." He looked at his watch and clucked his tongue. "I must be going now. It's been nice visiting with you. And really, I wouldn't sell the Bible until you've read in it. It may be more priceless than you realize."

He turned and walked away, leaving William, the banker, somewhat confused and annoyed. William met his children's need for approval by smiling in their direction and then headed his own little parade of one and marched from the school.

CHAPTER 22

The Color of His Eyes

THAT HALLOWEEN MORNING, three dreamers awoke with the stunning knowledge that they had all gathered on a certain green hillside and listened to the words of a most extraordinary man. Charles, Dory, and Nancy had not only sat in that throng of believers in their dreams but had also recognized one another, greeted one another, and felt the closeness of those who were living a miracle.

When Dory arrived at the bookshop after school, she greeted Charles with moist eyes. Her mind had strayed from her schoolwork the whole day as she relived the marvel of her dream. She had been transported to another time, another continent, and the experience was incredible. More than that, she had felt a rebirth, a hope that she was important, worthwhile in this world, someone more than an insignificant orphan child. Looking at Charles and Nancy last night, she knew she had made a tremendous difference in their lives; that because of her, events unfolded in such a way that the

Bibles were not thrown away, that the living messages were being read.

Charles had grasped the same realization. Now, as they began to discuss their experience, Nancy Rutledge rushed through the shop door, her children in breathless pursuit, still dressed in Halloween costumes.

"You children go find some nice books to look at," she told them. "Mommy has things to talk about with her friends."

Nancy's eyes met Dory's, and she quickly covered her mouth to stifle a short cry. She turned away from the children, not wanting to upset them. "It wasn't a dream, was it?" she whispered to Charles and Dory. "We were all there, weren't we? I can tell you what you were wearing and where we were all sitting." She closed her eyes, remembering. "I can tell you what color his eyes are and how soft he speaks, and still we could all hear him." Her voice broke. She could no longer express herself. Dory's eyes filled with tears, and she took Nancy's hand.

Charles was at a loss. He did not want to be forward enough to actually embrace these two gentle people, but at the moment, he felt closer to them than to anyone else in the world. Instead, he merely patted them both on the shoulder and wiped his own eyes. Nancy regained her speech.

"This is a miracle," she continued. "Oh, if only Jack could have read it. If he could have dreamed with me, things would have been different." She gazed at her children, and tears welled again. The spirit of forgiveness was working inside her. The words and their meaning had struck Nancy's heart that night. Regret and bitterness were beginning to melt in her, and she could embark on the process of compassion for Jack.

Charles was dumbstruck. He knew immediately that he and Greta must read together. It would mark a turning point for them, as it had for Nancy. Dory was thinking more and more of the others who owned the precious Bibles. "Mr. C., should we tell the others? Do you suppose anyone else has read yet?"

"My guess is that when they do, we will see them in the bookshop right away," Charles said, and then he began to chuckle. "If Theo reads, it will knock his socks off, him being the biggest heretic in town."

Nancy's children had abandoned their books. They made their way to the corner of the bookshop where Nancy and her friends huddled.

"Are you okay, Mommy?" The boy watched his mother anxiously. "I saw you crying."

"I'm just fine," she assured him. "I guess we'd better get you ready to go trick or treating, eh?"

Charles smiled enthusiastically. "You know, when I was a boy, we called it beggar's night. We all dressed up like hoboes, and we'd say, 'Tonight is beggar's night, and we have come to beg a bite.' Sometimes people gave us pennies instead of candy. You come by my house tonight, and I'll see what I can find in my piggy bank."

After Nancy and the children were gone, Dory busied herself sweeping the ever-present leaves from the doorway of the shop. She noticed a much-preoccupied woman at a standstill in front of the library, staring in her direction. It was Lottie Mariah. Books of all sizes and uncounted numbers balanced in her two arms, weighing her down significantly. Dory wondered why she did not fall under her load.

"Do you need help carrying those books?" she called across the square.

"What?" Lottie answered.

Dory trotted across the small park to repeat her question. This time Lottie answered directly. "What I need is help understanding them."

"What kind of books are they?"

"Dream books, mostly. Some are on visions and stuff like that."

"Oh," Dory said, not wanting to appear nosy but bristling with curiosity. "We have some books about dreams in the bookstore. They might be helpful."

Lottie shifted the weight of her stack an inch or so and looked above her at the sky. "What I don't need, kid, is more books. Well, I don't suppose you'd know much about the subject yourself, being young and all. I guess I might need a little assist here with these, though. Maybe I checked out too many."

"I'll just tell Mr. C. He won't mind. Nothing's happening at the store anyway."

"Swell," said Lottie. "Hurry back. My arms are about broke!"

"She must have read something!" Charles was excited at what Dory told him. "While you're walking with her, see if she says anything about the Bible. The old bookseller said there were people in town who desperately needed the messages in gold ink. Miss Mariah must surely be one of them. Another thing I wonder, and we ought to check on, is whether all the Bibles are exactly the same. We know that yours, mine, and Nancy's all have the Sermon on the Mount printed in gold. If you could get into her house and sneak a peek at her Bible—" Charles interrupted himself, taken aback. "I sound like some kind of detective. On the other hand, what if the others have read and nothing has happened?"

"Yeah. What if it's just the three of us on some kind of wave length or something. People might think we're nuts." A pause. "Do you think we're nuts, Mr. C.?"

"If you and I and Nancy are nuts, as you say, then we are nuts in the best way possible. No, Dory. I think we are being taught things we need to know. Now you'd better scoot before Miss Mariah comes apart at the seams."

Dory bounded briskly across the street and assumed some of Lottie's literary burden. On the way to her place, Lottie and Dory made small talk about how quickly the summer had gone, about the long, warm autumn, and about the many spooks populating lawns all over town.

"When I was young," said Lottie, "I did not much care for Halloween. My daddy always found some way to ruin it.

Now I really get a kick out of the little kids and the whole feeling. It kind of draws everything in, you know, before winter comes. I like the fall myself. Sometimes I walk out to the fields at the edge of town and just stare at the corn-stalks still standing. They remind me of little old ladies with dry, white hair blowing. And I like the sound of their leaves crackling in the wind."

"Yeah. I think they kind of look like arms waving at the crows."

"You ever see those big fat bugs that crawl into the corn ears? One time I yanked the husk off an ear, and a huge, hairy one oozed out. It made my ears buzz something awful. Took me years to ever eat another kernel of corn."

Dory shivered, remembering the pulsing shape and the buzzing in her own ears. She wondered if Lottie had felt it or knew about the gray, ominous thing that followed the Bibles.

"Here we are," said Lottie, turning sharply in front of her home. Dory was immediately taken with the place. An old gingerbread model, it boasted a verandah lined with potted, fading geraniums. A comfortable glider sat on the side porch, flanked by two wicker chairs and planter boxes.

"What a great place to read in the summer," she mused aloud. Lottie pushed the unlocked door open and allowed Dory to pass inside first. "Just dump the books down on that love seat there." Inside Lottie's parlor, Dory spotted the Bible immediately. It lay half concealed by the magazines, but there was no mistaking it. She decided to take a direct approach. "Gee, I have an old Bible that looks just like this one. Does yours have gold printing?"

Lottie looked up sharply. Her dream flashed through her mind. "Yeah. Some of it looks like gold. Not everything, but some of the stories are like that. I bought it at your bookstore a while back, for my clients, mostly churchgoing ladies."

Dory leafed through the musty pages. She stopped in the book of Matthew. There it was, just as in her book, the

Sermon in gold. She ventured a brief comment. "I read this one. You know, the old bookseller told Mr. C. that the gold printing makes the stories come to life. Have you read any of them yet?"

Lottie began to perspire slightly. She had no wish to share her dream with this girl. "Uh, no," she lied. "Maybe when I finish all of these, I'll get to it." She picked up two of the library volumes and studied their covers. The hint was direct enough for Dory, who said she must be going. Lottie thanked her by insisting she take a bottle of root beer for her trouble and saw her through the door.

That phrase the girl used, where had she heard it before? Oh, yes, just yesterday, from the undertaker. He had said it nearly same way. Well, he and the bookseller were right on the money about this one. If ever a story came to life for her, the one she read last night had. She hoped to find an explanation for the experience, because in spite of the strong emotions it evoked, her involvement with the spiritual was limited. She felt she must discover a reasonable, sane, and sound explanation for the phenomenon. She was certain she could locate similar accounts in at least one of these books.

As she peered through the contents of the first volume, Lottie was distracted by a memory of her dream. Something specific about the man came to her over and over.

It was his eyes, the color of them, the gentle strength in his gaze that she saw. She lay back and immersed herself in the memory and the dream, and in the color of his eyes. The library books went unopened that afternoon.

CHAPTER 23

Tricks and Treats

THE ANDERSON SISTERS asked Nancy and the children to drop by their house on their trick or treat rounds that night. "Be sure you come here last, and then we can visit before you go home." Nancy could not refuse the women, who were fast becoming friends.

Adele continued. "I like to dress up a bit myself to greet the little ones at the door. This year I have a biblical costume. Of course, the children won't recognize me as Elizabeth, but she's a woman I've always admired. She had a baby at a very advanced age, you know."

"Wouldn't that be strange? Being your age and having a new baby. Oh, I didn't mean . . ." Nancy began to stumble over her words. "I'm sorry. That sounded rude. What I meant was . . ."

Adele laughed. "Oh, it's all right. I'm used to my age by now, and yes, I do think it would be difficult having a new baby at this point in life. I'm content to admire your children from afar. Please don't forget to come by."

October's hazy, ochre luster soon withdrew from the day, and darkness fell. Scores of goblins and legendaries tumbled onto the pavement, hurled from their homes by the force of Halloween itself. Johnny Appleseed, Paul Bunyan, and Peter Rabbit took up the sidewalk trail beside Draculae aplenty. Black-clad witches danced behind Cinderella and the Frog Prince. Night birds, perched high above the scuttling revelers, watched with critical and trenchant expressions. Riotous paraders below muffled the scamper and rustling of dinner mice in the open yards, as they scurried for safety beneath back porches.

Adele, the biblical Elizabeth, passed out homemade cookies in little paper bags. Her soft-textured sugar cookies decorated with orange frosting were a perennial favorite in the neighborhood. This had been a good day for the ladies. After tutoring Nancy in the morning, they mixed cookie dough and chilled it in the icebox. They made several calls to shut-ins from the church, and then they put the finishing touches on their porch decorations and baked dozens of sweet-smelling rounds.

As the darkness slipped through their windows, the sisters waited for the quivering of the loosely wired doorbell. Various versions of fairy tale characters introduced themselves from the other side of the screen door and held out gaping maws of bottomless pillowcases. At precisely eight o'clock, Nancy and her children approached the Anderson home, laughing and celebrating the mild evening. The two sisters welcomed them graciously and invited the family to come inside. By now, the hordes of miniature beggars had thinned out considerably, and they could visit a while. Ardis reached into her oversized papier-mâché pumpkin, pulled out two large brown bags stuffed with holiday treats, and then shushed Nancy's slight protests. The children were delirious.

"How do you like my costume? I feel absolutely biblical in it." Adele twirled herself around, swishing the long, plentiful robes above her sandals. She was proud of her costume, and it showed. Her enthusiasm did not spread to Nancy. Nancy had seen for herself the clothing worn in times of old. The colors were all wrong, and even the drape of the robe was inaccurate. She weighed sharing this information with the good old woman. She decided against it and mustered a positive reply. "I can see where you would feel biblical. It looks nice on you." This satisfied Adele, and Nancy assured herself that it was not a lie.

After a short visit, Nancy and the children left for home. When her small brood was settled under warm quilts, Nancy went to the cupboard and retrieved her Bible. Caressing its worn cover, she weighed whether to read that night. The reassurance from Charles that if the Bible were kept indoors calmed her as she recalled Dory's account of the shapeless thing that followed the books. She shivered at the night wind now moaning beneath the creaking eaves. She decided to go directly to bed to rest for tomorrow's duties.

Outside, a frustrated force circled the house in aggravation. The apparition trailed mist and odor and added its lament to the whispers in the wind. Finally, frustrated by thwarted efforts, it dissipated and wafted to the cemetery. As for the others who were in possession of the ancient scriptures, Halloween passed in other ways.

Lottie had gussied herself up in the most outrageous of queenly dress. She wore a tiara of dime-store paste, her throat and wrists dripped with costume jewelry, and her royal gown sparkled with hundreds of hand-sewn sequins. She burned candles on the porch and throughout her parlor. The result was that a soft, lustrous aura surrounded her. Dressed this way, Lottie came as close to looking angelic as she ever had. The treats she passed out were a success, and the yard decor was a delight to children and parents as well. She was the object of many friendly overtures and returned smile for smile. That night, at last feeling warm and accepted in her own hometown, Lottie decided she might challenge herself to more change. She dared to read again, this time from the Old Testament.

William Hicken buried himself in a different sort of book and refused to answer the door for anyone. Since his wife had taken their children out, William put the treat box on the step, and the first ten beggars who came along cleaned it out. There is no honor system connected with such a night. In fact, upon finding the box empty and the house dark, some of the older and more shameless boys gave the Hicken home a proper egging.

Charles, much to Greta's chagrin, passed out money. He hollowed the innards of his penny bank by dumping all the coppers onto the floor and dividing them into piles of ten. For Nancy's children, he built penny stacks as high as they would stand and then added coins to amount to one dollar each. Greta growled over his extravagance. "Every little cent adds up," she reminded him. "Children would just as soon have popcorn or peppermint sticks, you know." Charles ignored her as only he knew how and passed out every paltry penny in the pig.

Dory's Aunt Ginny had put her in charge of feeding the holiday brigade. "You may oversee the doorbell ritual," she moaned. "I'm too old to be jumping up and down all night." Dory enjoyed it. After all, few years had gone by since she marched up and down the warmly lit streets in her own Halloween finery.

At Theo's home, nothing out of the ordinary happened. Nothing at all, so we leave it at that. However, events at the mortuary more than made up for a routine thirty-first at home.

When you are fifteen-year-old boys, you are too old to trick or treat. The turning over of outhouses is impossible, since most of them are well guarded in a small town. Three such young men were out on their annual spook spree and made the witless decision to break into Theo's place of business. The boys have long since gone to their own rest, but everyone has known their kind; some have even been like them.

"Old man Atwood's had it coming for years," one of the boys growled. Come to think of it, he may have had a name. Perhaps it was Parker.

The boys decided to enter the building through a window off the side alley. "Nobody's dead in there. Only your grandpa died in the last week. Anyway, the new undertaker gets the newest ones."

"You got your flashlight?"

"Yep. Say, what are we gonna do when we get in?"

"Let's open up all the coffins and dump stuff in 'em. Trash and stuff."

"That's stupid. We gotta do something really disgusting."

"What? Like put your sister's picture in one?"

There was a slight scuffle. "Lay off my sister, okay?"

"Okay, okay! What can we do? It's gotta be something he'll hate."

"I got it, I got it!" The Parker boy was suddenly inspired by stories from his father's youth. "We round up all the cats we can find. We stick 'em into caskets and close the lids. They die, swell up overnight, and stink to high heaven. Atwood opens 'em in the morning, and holy cats!"

Smiles all around put a stamp of approval on the plan. Their dilemma became apparent when the boys could only find one unprotected cat in the surrounding neighborhood— one cat, and a white one at that. Well, they decided, one would have to do.

Jimmying the window was not difficult, since not many people attempt to break into a mortuary, and certainly none attempt to break out. The boys easily entered that dark world of morbid chemistry, where embalming miracles are performed and lifeless hairs are slicked down by a man who is definitely not a barber. Inside, the air hung stale like mummy's breath. Its oppressiveness nearly smothered their mischievous intent.

"Jeez! Who beefed it?" gagged one of them.

Mustering courage, they stumbled through the room—it was Theo's office—and down a wide hall. At the end of the passageway was a broad metal door. Years ago, Theo, as a prankster himself, had scratched the word *clientele* in the metal. He and his father had made a good joke of it at the time and decided to let it stay. The three boys were not amused and recoiled in the opposite direction.

They arrived at a coffin display room, where they saw five versions of the dreaded oblong box. This room was as stuffy as the first but was made worse by the odor of mothballs emanating from a closet in the corner. By now, the cat was becoming restless in its canvas bag and nearly got away from the boys.

"We gotta dump him now, or he'll scratch my arm off."

"Okay, then. Which one are we gonna put him in?"

"First one you open," said the cat-boy.

"Who says I gotta open it? I opened the window."

The unspoken fear, of course, was that one of the caskets held the remains of some unknown stiff. Their eyes rested on the third boy, the Parker boy, whose idea the whole thing was. "Well, sure! I ain't afraid to open one." His voice quavered only slightly. His eyes darted from one box to another, as if he were making some sort of scientific study. "Aw, I don't know. Just spin me around a couple times and then I'll point."

The boys were in the middle of the third spin when they heard a scratching and shuffling sound from the window in the back of the room.

"What's that?" demanded the spinner.

"It ain't your grandma, dopey!" replied cat-boy. "Just open one and let's beat it!"

Blindly, the Parker boy lunged toward a casket and lifted the lid. Cat-boy pitched the screeching animal, canvas bag and all, into the black pit, and they ran for the door. The boys made a wrong turn in the hall and headed toward the front entry. In their rush, they failed to wonder why the door was already open. Stumbling through the hall, they knocked over Theo's entry desk. The old Bible and an empty vase fell with it. The Bible thumped, and the vase shattered and splintered into an array of tiny shards. The rascals' flashlight bounced along the floor, its beams reflecting bits of glass in a billion little prisms. The tattered scriptures popped off the toe of the Parker boy's tennis shoe and landed within inches of the wide-open door.

The first boy to see the pulsating, cold mass waiting outside leaped silently back into the vestibule, fright sticking sideways in his throat like a fish bone. The other two roared past him on a dead run and never looked back. Within a few short minutes, a passing pedestrian peered innocently into the open door and assured the frightened boy that nothing was there. "Must have been somebody dressed up for Halloween, son."

CHAPTER 24

Aftermath

THE PUDGY DEPUTY put together the pieces of the funeral parlor puzzle quickly. The pedestrian who had reassured the boy that there was no monster outside Atwood's Mortuary had also dragged him to the police station and reported the break-in. Of course, he wished he had not done so, after the panicky juvenile named his own son as an accomplice. The following day, damage to the funeral home was assessed and punishment assigned. No one paid much attention to the monster tale even though all three of the adolescents supported it. Theo laughed it off as wild imaginings or the result of sipping cooking wine. He threatened to have the boys wash the next cadaver that came his way, and the Parker boy nearly fainted.

Word of their escapades sped through the school and got to Dory quickly. She and Charles discussed it once more just before closing time. "It looks like the thing is still after a Bible, Mr. C. I'm sure that's what the boys saw."

Charles nodded in solemn agreement. Just then the brass bells over the door jingled, and William Hicken walked in. He was full of research and raring to make money from Charles's poor judgment.

"I'm looking for more of those Bibles," he announced. "Are there any others for sale? Surely there were more."

"Indeed, there were. Unfortunately, or fortunately for myself, they are all gone," Charles answered, somewhat wary and feeling protective of the precious volumes. "Have you had a chance to read anything in yours?"

"Read? No, not really. I'm interested in them as collector's items." He lied through his very small teeth, twenty-five remaining, to be exact. He had always considered men like Charles to be rubes of sorts, unsophisticated, bound to be poor for life, and appallingly meek. One little fabrication to a natural chump was not so bad. "Well, have you an address or telephone number for the gentleman who sold them to you?"

Even if I did, thought Charles, *I don't believe I'd give it to you.* "No," he replied aloud. "The fellow just blew through here with the wind, so to speak, and disappeared."

William was becoming exasperated. Now the tiresome job of running down any other copies faced him. "Would you mind giving me the names of those who bought them? I do know that Theo Atwood has one. How many more were there?"

Charles looked at Dory, and she returned his glance knowingly. "Well, I have one myself, and I'm keeping it. Collector's item, you know."

Just as he finished his sentence, Lottie burst through the door. She was breathless. "I can't believe this! The first time was fantastic enough, but last night! Last night I saw that Moses man, like he was coming out of a cloud off the mountain! Where in the world did that Bible come from?"

William looked at Lottie. His lips curled into an oily smile. Charles nervously tried to quiet her. In her excitement, she was oblivious to his signals. She went on. "And do you know who I saw there? You can't believe it! Nancy Rutledge, in the flesh! The stories are so real!" Suddenly, she looked at William, as if seeing him for the first time. She saw the expressions of dismay on Charles's and Dory's faces. "Oh, I—maybe I should come back later," she stuttered.

"It's all right," said Charles. His manner was smooth as cream. He moved toward the door and opened it, gesturing to William. "Mr. Hicken was just leaving. I'll let you know, William, if I come across any more such volumes. Good-bye, now."

William was in shock. Never had Charles brushed him off so rudely. *These Bibles must be worth even more than I figured,* he thought. Pondering as he walked, he concluded that buying them from Theo and the hairdresser would be simple but getting the one away from Charles might take a little more capital.

"Maybe Charles is not as dumb as I thought" he said aloud, rounding the corner to the bank. It was nearly dark now. He heard footsteps behind him but paid little attention. When he arrived at the bank, he pulled out his key to open the locked door. Bank employees were not fond of staying past closing hours, so the door was already secured. A hand tapped him gently on the shoulder, startling him slightly. For a split second, he thought perhaps it was Charles, reconsidering. He turned to see a very pale man, wearing a heavy, dark, knee-length cape and other curious clothing. The man's suit looked to be at least fifty years old, his hat sat high upon his head, and the shoes buttoned on the side. He smelled of unwashed skin and unidentifiable exhalation. William stepped quickly back, an electric chill ran through him. He shivered, unable to classify the slight fear he felt.

"Yes, what it it?" he demanded.

"Mr. Hicken?"

"Who are you?"

"I am someone like yourself, interested in antique Bibles."

"I only have the one. I'm going to be selling it soon. What

is your business with Bibles? Are you the man who sold the old Bibles to Charles?"

"Oh, Charles, that milquetoast? Hardly. My business is to help you turn a profit. You have an interest in turning a profit, do you not? I also know who has the other Bibles."

"How would you know that? For some reason, Charles seems to be secretive about it."

"I know anything I need to know. I would like to strike a bargain with you. I can pay you twice what you would get from antique dealers anywhere in the world if you can get the other five Bibles for me."

William trembled at the thought. "You have their names? Are they here in town? There are five more? Who has them?"

"Let us first speak of bargains. Name me your price. Get me the Bibles, and I will reward you fittingly. Return to this spot tomorrow at the same time."

William was eager to pursue this avenue of exchange. "I can have amounts by tomorrow morning. Why don't you drop by my office then?"

"Tomorrow morning I am occupied. No, it will be as I said. Tomorrow evening, same time, same place. Good-night, then." The man flung the cape around his narrow shoulders and swept away. His long legs protruded insect-like from beneath the black frock coat. William fancied the man resembled a cricket—a very pale, very extinct cricket.

CHAPTER 25

Visions

I T WAS LATER that evening while Charles was searching
his volumes for the elusive gold ink information that his
second encounter with the seller of books occurred. He was
deep in thought and research, his back toward the door. He
had locked up securely, he was sure, yet suddenly the bells
sounded, and he felt a draft sweep the shop. He turned, half
expecting to see Dory or Greta. Instead, he was greeted by
the old man, once again dressed in rags and raising dust from
the floor. He stood in the middle of the room, his tatters falling softly over the worn shoes.

"You're back!" Charles leaped to his feet and felt an odd
rush of relief. "What is it? What causes the dreams?" Only
after a moment did he ask, "How did you get in? The door
was locked."

"Last question answered first," said the ragged vagabond,
always answering the same way. "I've been here a while. You
just haven't seen me. What causes the dreams, the reactions,

the visions, whatever you wish to call them? What do you think of them, Charles?"

Charles sighed in wonder. "Oh, they are fantastic! Unbelievable! Yet they feel so real. Why the first time I read, I was swept away. I was in shock, still I didn't want the feeling to end. I've read more than once, you know."

"It's not poison in the ink, let me assure you," the strange man said. "That's what you want to know, isn't it? Every reader brings himself to the pages. What you dream is what you are, or what you might become. The others are dreaming, are they not? What about Bill Hicken and Theo Atwood? You must do everything within your power to get them to read. It is their only salvation. Do it, Charles! You have the calling."

"Wait a minute! Those men are not just lukewarm Christians, you know. They are out-and-out anti-church; they laugh at religion. Bill is trying to collect all of the Bibles, probably for money. Theo is lost already; everyone knows that."

"Everyone *thinks* that," the bookseller emphatically corrected Charles. "I don't think that, and neither should you. Better go home now, Charles." He turned to walk away and then stopped momentarily. "And by the way, it doesn't matter where your novels are. Just concentrate on the Bibles. Greta will come around."

Charles's mind was reeling. How did the man know all of these things? A book slipped from his grip, and he stooped to retrieve it. When he looked up, the old seller of books was gone. Somehow, his encounter with the bookseller, though unsettling in some respects, calmed his mind, and he felt reassured for himself and the other readers.

Very quickly, the three dreamers conspired to read another of the stories printed in gold. They drew Lottie into their circle, a circle she had unwittingly entered when she'd rushed into the bookshop, blurting out her experience with the wonders of reading.

"I haven't told anyone about the Bible, though," she assured them. Somehow she knew that the little group wished to retain their extraordinary secret a bit longer.

"Theo Atwood and Bill Hicken are the only others with Bibles," said Charles. "They may have read something."

Lottie snorted and moved to the obvious. "A bear in the woods would be more likely to read the Bible than either of those two!" she remarked. "What about your wife?" she asked Charles.

"Greta? She thinks my copy went out with the poor box. I'm almost ashamed to say I've been reading it in secret."

"Oh, I would never have read mine in front of Jack either," Nancy interjected, her eyes wide with understanding. "He would have thrown it out too!"

"Well, Jack isn't a problem now, so you can do whatever you want." Suddenly out of her usual gruff, sharp-tongued character, Lottie put her arm around Nancy's shoulder and offered an affectionate squeeze. Until now, Dory had been silent. She had been searching her memory for an appropriate story for the group. When there was a lull in the conversation, she spoke quietly. "I think that it would be exciting to go to Egypt and see the parting of the Red Sea. Maybe we all have that printed in gold."

"Dory," Charles gently chided his young employee, "I don't think we should think of it as actually going there. True, it *is* an amazing feeling, but somehow, even though it seems so real, it can't be any more than a dream."

"Can't it be a vision?" she answered him with a question. "People in old times had visions, and they thought of those as more than dreams. They even predicted the future with them. How could they see the future without going there, at least in their minds?"

"Or in their spirits." Nancy surprised them all with this statement. "When I was a little girl, I was sure that your spirit could escape from your body, and you would be able to go to places and do things that your body would keep you from doing. In fact, I used to do that when Jack was mean and ornery, you know, just travel outside yourself. That's how those dreams seem to me."

"I say the kid has a point and so does Nancy." Lottie jumped up from her seat in the shop and reached for the nearest book. "Look here! I've read a lot of stuff in my life, mostly made-up books and gossip sheets, and I never once dreamed about *those* stories. I feel just like you do." She spoke directly to Dory. "When I dreamed, it was exactly like being there. It was more real than my own house, in a way. It was like somewhere I had been before. I knew what was on the streets and who was around me and even the smells were familiar. When he spoke to me—" Lottie's eyes suddenly filled with tears, and her lip trembled slightly. She swallowed hard, trying desperately to pull herself together. Wiping the tears with a handkerchief offered by Charles, she cleared her throat and then merely nodded her head. "It was real, all right. And it was something I needed."

"Perhaps you're right," said Charles. He did not wish to make the reality of the dreams a point of contention, after all. Dory offered to go to Nancy's home to look up the story for her, but Nancy refused her help. "Thanks anyway, but I know I'll recognize it when I see it. Are we reading tonight, then?"

"We are!" said Lottie.

"Well then, I say, read on MacDuff, read on!" Charles beamed at his humorous play on Shakespeare. The readers did not seem impressed but chuckled politely and bid a collective good-bye to the group.

So it was that the four readers traveled that night on their separate conveyances to the same destination. Dressed in the coarse fabric of the Israelites, surrounded by the thousands who followed Moses from the land of Egypt, Charles, Dory, Lottie, and Nancy recognized one another in yet another fantastic nocturnal flight. They were guided by the pillar of cloud by day and the pillar of fire by night. Fresh in their minds were remembrances of the recent plagues that beleaguered the Pharaoh and his people. Also fresh in their thoughts were the complaints of many around them. Scores of Israelites wished to return to Egypt rather than wander in the wilderness. They came to know for themselves the sweet taste of manna that descended like the morning dew every day. They found themselves encamped on the shores of the Red Sea and worrying about the Egyptians who followed close behind. All that night a strong east wind blew, casting the waters of the Red Sea aside and causing the dry land to appear. It was as a forty-year-long night, a lifetime association with the biblical wanderers, and it solidified the dreamers once more.

Thus, as Nancy's children cuddled warmly together, as Greta slept and dreamed of nothing, as Dory's Aunt Ginny snored softly in her bed, as Lottie's cat lay snuggled next to his mistress's feet, the readers adventured together in a vision, or in spirit. When each one awoke the following morning, it did not matter whether vision or dream or spirit had transported them; each knew that the experience had been real. Now it was their task to discover what they were learning from all this.

CHAPTER 26

Resurrection

IT HAPPENED THAT in Theo's Bible there were twenty-two scriptural quotations printed in gold ink and two longer narratives. Twenty of them dealt with the resurrection of the dead, another one told the more familiar and beloved Nativity story, and the last related the dark and ominous story of betrayal and Calvary. Theo had probably heard a few of those quotations during his lifetime and certainly had been subjected to portions of the birth in Bethlehem by osmosis. With the yearly encroachment of commercialism on the Christmas celebration, he had felt some obligation to hang a wreath here and there. Greeting cards, however, were out of the question. He could not bring himself to go that far.

None of the vague memories of the promises of resurrection struck him, except in a pessimistic way. His treatise on the non-smoking angel theory was widely known. When he reported property damage to the sheriff following the pranksters' escapades, he noted that the side window had been jimmied but could be locked, the white cat had shredded one of his cheaper casket linings, and a vase was broken. His Bible was retrieved from its resting place near the door and dusted off to be placed back on the table.

November first came in on a decidedly cold wind that year. As if shivered off by the trees themselves, all the leaves had abandoned their twigs and branches and swirled, dead and aimless, in the chill. The overcast sky allowed only the slightest tinge of rose to appear on the eastern horizon and soon covered that as well.

Theo had rarely been affected adversely by weather, but this particular day settled like a dead weight in his chest. The full force of this solemnity struck him when he saw his five empty caskets. Suddenly, he felt nearly as hollow as the boxes that lay mutely before him. He tried to shrug the emotion away. Out loud, he repeated the bawdiest joke he knew, but the gloomy inner man did not laugh. In short, he felt as though the very marrow of himself was being sucked away. What was wrong?

"It must be that new man taking my business," he thought. Upon reflection, however, he noted that deaths had fallen off since Mr. Angell came. Aside from old man Anderson, little Dickie Parker's father, and Jack Rutledge, the Grim Reaper had not drawn anyone into his dark cloak. Theo walked through the front door of his mortuary and stood gazing out onto the street. He had replaced the Bible on the table next to his box of business cards. The book was closed, and its worn cover bespoke years of use by others—all fools according to Theo. An errant breeze rushed through the open doorway, flapping the old, thin pages. The soft rustle of paper called his attention to the book, and he left off staring at the gray day. Closing the door, he noticed how the gold ink glowed from the book leaves. He had not paid attention to them before, not even after William Hicken had tried to buy the Bible from him. Now he was lured to them, as if by some unknown persuasion. Theo began to read.

How strange it was. The passages began: "Then there were two thieves crucified with him, one on the right hand and another on the left." Several verses later, the highlighted declaration ended in this way: "And the graves were opened; and many bodies of the saints which slept arose, and came out of the graves after his resurrection, and went into the holy city, and appeared unto many."

There was no immediate reaction from Theo, except a possible shiver, caused, he thought, by the wind. He turned his attention to more worldly and familiar aims. For no explainable reason, he slipped the Bible into his pocket when he locked up. He was puffing furiously on his accustomed see-gar while he walked through the darkened neighborhood. Behind him, rushing on a cabalistic wind, was the odious mist that had followed Dory. It was the same ghoulish shape that had frightened the wits out of William Hicken. Theo was oblivious to the thing behind him. The draught had become frigid, and so any chill that overcame him was the fault of that wind. Any stench that preceded the shape was overcome by the strong odor of his own cigar. He arrived home completely unaffected by the thing that hovered so eagerly at his heels. At the end of that long and boring day, Theo Atwood crawled into his bed and, unable to sleep, opened the book once more. After reading, he slept and began his own journey into the land of dreamers.

His awakening the next morning was abrupt. He was sweating profusely, and his heart pounded furiously beneath his well-padded ribs. Like Ebeneezer Scrooge, Theo ran to his window and opened it to the morning. The agitated mortician swallowed air as if he were a drowning man and, after a few seconds, slumped into a nearby armchair.

"Great Holy Moses!" he cried aloud. He was still trembling and weak from the shock of his dream. He searched his hands meticulously and in vain for signs of blood. Our mortician saw that he wore pajamas, the same ones he had put on last evening at bedtime. His feet were bare, not sandaled as they were during the night. He felt his head for the metal helmet and reached to his side, seeking a sword.

"Then I wasn't there! I didn't do it!" he whispered frantically, hoping to be relieved of his imagined crime. Still, he was gripped by the belief that he had seen, encouraged, and participated in that horrible act. He had never imagined a crucifixion, not once in his life given a thought to the appalling punishment of old times. Now he awoke to the stain of it, to the conviction that he had been a part of *the Crucifixion itself!* Theo feared, but for what? Perhaps his sanity. He was so unaccustomed to things spiritual that he could only conclude that he was losing his mind. It was that story! The passages in that abominable Bible had nearly driven him mad. "Well," Theo bellowed hoarsely, "if old Bill wants it so bad, he can have it!" Theo would replace the book with a brand new one and never crack its cover. After a few more minutes passed, he picked up the phone and called William Hicken's home.

CHAPTER 27

November 2

ARDIS AND ADELE were pleased with their protege's progress. Nancy still held her silence about the Bible, and minding the warnings from Charles and Dory, she kept the book high in her cupboard. The sisters had arranged three housecleaning jobs for her, so she was busily beginning to earn her own way. So much had changed in the short time since Jack's death that Nancy was still in a slight daze. Life was becoming something invigorating and warm, though the signs of the season promised a cold winter. She felt a sense of excitement now about Christmas and the New Year. The little celebrations in her life would no longer include ugly scenes and unexplained rages. Peace was now a part of her life. Reading was opening the window to a different world, and the gold scriptures were reaching deep inside her.

On the other side of town, William Hicken was pleased with himself since he was about to be the possessor of not one, but two of the precious volumes this second day of

November. It was odd that Theo called him this morning, curiously eager to relinquish his Bible now. Just a few days ago, he had been reluctant to let it go. William wondered what had changed Theo's mind.

"It's just that I decided to bag that idea and go with a brand-new one," Theo had explained. "Besides, it got even more beat up in the break-in the other night. Well, not so bad that an antique dealer wouldn't want it, for sure. I paid a couple of bucks for it, but you can have it for nothing. I'll drop it off later today."

Theo's words came in a rush, and he hung up the telephone without a good-bye or kiss-my-foot, contrary to his usual habit. William now calculated that the other Bibles might fall to him as easily and made some long-distance calls to dealers to get a feel for the going market. His plan was to ask the mysterious, pale man for one hundred percent more, just to see what would happen. The man had indicated that William could name his price, and he would pay it. It had not yet occurred to the banker to ask why the gentleman did not just go directly to the Bible owners. Greed was blinding his sensibilities. Playing the middleman suited him and his covetous nature. William was being led unawares down a path that, in the end, would yield little satisfaction and much disappointment.

It was after five o'clock by the time Theo could leave his business for the bank. The minutiae of a mortician's life occupied part of his day, and the remainder was spent alternately trying to grasp the meaning of his dream and to rid his mind of it. William had assured Theo that he would wait. Theo grabbed the Bible on his way out and locked the mortuary door securely behind him. As his footsteps sounded on the cold, gray pavement, the chill of early evening played about his face and ears. He drew up his shoulders and moved at a speedier pace. Theo was suddenly uneasy. His heartbeat increased as he recalled the dread of the morning, awakening from his dream as he had, with a start. The same sickening feeling enveloped him. It seemed that the very life of the brisk autumn air was quickly extinguishing. Had he looked over his shoulder, he might have seen the reason, for hovering a few yards behind Theo's rushing figure was the gray pulsation that had visited him the night before, closing in on him swiftly. This time it was stronger. This time Theo had a weakness, and the thing could penetrate his fears.

Theo perceived the stifling feeling to come from possessing the old Bible. There was something about it, he was sure, that caused last night's voodoo. In his rush to reach the bank and be rid of the cursed book of scripture, he turned the corner and collided dead on with Mr. T. T. Angell. The mass behind came to a vaporous, skidding halt.

"Great Holy Christmas!" Theo shouted, unable to control his shock. "You nearly scared me spitless!" When he realized it was Mr. Angell, he backed down slightly. "That is, I didn't expect to be plowed under by a fellow undertaker."

T. T. Angell, recovered from the collision, smiled. "Well, Mr. Atwood, when your time comes, you don't expect to bury yourself, do you? You seem to be in a rush."

"I ain't in a rush to die, if that's what you're saying!" Theo said, defensively, instantly suspicious of Mr. Angell's concern.

"I merely wondered if you were being pursued. You act as if the devil himself were chasing you."

"Wouldn't that just please the socks off you! For your information, Mr. High and Mighty, I'm taking this worthless piece of junk to Hicken. He thinks it's worth a lot of money, and he can sell it for big bucks." Theo waved the Bible in Mr. Angell's face.

"What do you really think of it, Theo?"

"I just told you! I think it's a worthless collection of fairy tales."

"Fairy tales? Then it is certainly not a thing to be feared, don't you think?"

Theo was stunned. How did Angell know that at the

bottom of his brashness there was fear? "Nobody said anything about being afraid. Say, I ain't afraid of anything; I just
don't want it lying around anymore." Angell's calm demeanor
further unnerved the shaken Theo. He then tried to push past
his nemesis. Mr. Angell showed remarkable strength for such
a lean-looking fellow and restrained him. Theo could not get
around him.

"Then give the Bible to me," said Angell. "I'll explain to
Mr. Hicken."

"You in the business of selling antiques yourself? Greedy
bunch, ain't you?" Theo shook himself free. He thought for
a brief moment and then thrust the book into Mr. Angell's
open hand. "Here! Take it! And good riddance. Explain it to
Bill yourself!" Then Theo scurried away, happy to be free of
the fabricator of his most unusual fright. When he arrived at
his darkened home, he bolted the door and switched on every
light in the room. After swallowing a couple of sleeping pills,
he put Mendelssohn on his Victrola and went to bed with a
lamp burning in the hall.

Subsequent to watching Theo hurry away, Mr. Angell
disappeared into a small shop off the square and waited for
the change he knew was coming. Around the corner, the gray
mass cursed Angell with dark irreverence and at once, under
cover of night, assumed the form of the tall, pale cricket. T. T.
Angell hid well behind the door and watched the stick man
glide past the shop window. The cloaked, translucent figure
went directly to the bank and waited for William.

It was almost five-thirty, and William was already
extremely peevish. He assumed now that Theo had changed
his mind. He was out of patience with the mortician, heap-
ing invectives on his nonmaterializing friend. Two Bibles
in the hand would have meant better leverage for William.
Perhaps, he thought wildly, *the cloaked man has already
gotten to Theo and bought the book directly from him.* Instantly,
he was doubly vexed with the ill-valued Theo. At the same
time William was cursing the poor man, he paced the

sidewalk, wishing he were a smoker. It would have given him something to do with his nervous hands. The banker peered into the dimly lit street and saw that the cloaked man approached. Aha! Well, anyway, he would now get the names of the others who had Bibles and ask if the stranger had bought Theo's copy already.

The man spoke to William immediately. Though he was several feet away, his cold voice carried across the distance, penetrating the banker's ear like a sharp, spun-glass thread, almost as if the words came from within William himself.

"Have you fixed a value on the books?" he asked, quite directly.

"I have," answered William and gave the man a cautiously outrageous sum. He would ask about Theo in a moment.

"All that for the six?" asked the cricket.

"You told me you could pay twice what the antique dealers would offer. That sum is two times what I could get on the market as it stands." William was going to remain adamant. The man appeared to back down somewhat. "Exactly. I did promise. When you deliver the six to me, you will be paid."

"Then you haven't bought Theo's Bible?"

"Theo Atwood is a fool. He has given his copy to the other undertaker in your pitiful town. I *nearly* had it . . ." The cricket's voice clicked and hissed sharply into William's ear. William shuddered and instinctively backed away.

"So then, who are the others who have the books?"

"Your stubborn bookshop owner, Charles, is one. The hairdresser, Lottie Mariah, is another. She only bought it as a mockery against her patrons. The simpering girl who works for Charles is a third. Her name is Dory. Dreadfully dull name, isn't it? Of course, Theo *was* the fourth, but now you'll have a time of it getting the book from the undertaker. The fifth is a widow who can barely read her own name. She's the Rutledge woman living on the other side of the cemetery. And you, my dear William, are the sixth."

William pictured each of the owners in his mind. These people should be easily bought off. Perhaps Charles might pose a problem, but the others would probably just as soon have brand new Bibles, Bibles with nice, shiny, gleaming, gold-leafed pages. He would offer them new Bibles, plus five dollars on top.

"When do you think you can deliver them to me?" The cricket shifted his elongated body beneath the ill-fitting cloak. The sound was like the crumpling of paper. His movement stirred a foul aroma in the air, and William backed farther away. Sensing William's not-so-subtle aversion, the cricket reached into the folds of his mantle and withdrew a large number of bills. These he fanned deftly before William's disbelieving eyes, creating the desired effect. He knew that William, out of avarice and contempt, would do everything in his power to deliver those Bibles. William was his.

CHAPTER 28

Eternal Conflict

"THE BATTLE IS joined again," wrote the undertaker T. T. Angell. "The lines are drawn and the ammunition is ready. In numbers there is strength, and it surely would have been good to have Theo with us. As it is, he wants nothing to do with the Bible. Perhaps he'll return when the moment is right. William will come to frustration over the matter, and I hope that he is not ruined in the end."

T. T. Angell sat at his desk, tapping his pen against the gold tooth that Lottie had seen the day before Halloween. Before him lay a chestnut-hued, dog-eared journal, whose pages bespoke frequent entries. He stopped writing for a moment to muse on the events that had occurred over the past few weeks. They were not so very different from those that had gone on before in unnumbered years. True, the people had different names, different occupations, but their stages of life were always similar. And they always had needs. Some needs were more dire than others. T. T. Angell considered Theo and William to be in grievous straits, neither of them being inclined to look beyond this world, either for their values or their inspiration.

"I fear the adversary has our banker in the clutches of his own greed. If William will only read a little, and the right verses, he will be able to recognize himself and make the change. My enemy always knows who to approach but has failed thus far to get these last six volumes in his grip."

The undertaker was reluctant to admit that he was down to six volumes. Time was when a whole village of individuals possessed their own Bibles. Oh, it only lasted a short while, but the result was wonderful. Each individual came to see himself not only for what he was, but for what he might become. However, the adversary was wily and did have certain powers. T. T. Angell knew that it agitated his enemy no end to have even those few volumes still circulating. He needed to snuff them all out, like six waxen altar candles, so that their light could no longer shine. The night he had visited Charles in the bookshop, T. T. Angell had hoped not to see the dark shadow that pursued him across centuries. He would like to have seen one group of people read, grow, and progress without the interference of that abomination. Still, a small voice whispered to him that it was part of the grand design: opposition, always opposition, before the greatest seasoning and development.

A knock at the door interrupted his thoughts. It was William.

"Mr. Angell. I wonder if I might take a few minutes of your time." William stood before him, passionate as a college freshman. His shining countenance did not fool T. T. Angell for a moment.

"Of course. I trust you do not require my professional services?"

"No, thankfully. I have come to inquire about an antique Bible. I believe Theo Atwood either sold it or gave it to you just this evening."

"Yes. Word travels quickly in a town this small. But how did you know, and what is it you want to know about the book?"

"Theo offered it to me earlier, and then we had a little disagreement. I would like to make you an offer for it. I am prepared to trade a brand-new one, plus a little cash, for the beat-up volume you have. You see, I'm a collector of antique books, and this one would add a lot to my permanent collection. It can't be of much value to you, and he did offer it to me first."

Lies, lies, lies. William was impounding his soul further with every word he uttered. T. T. Angel smiled quietly and answered the banker confidently. "I too am a collector. I do not wish to trade or sell the Bible. I'm afraid my answer is no."

William, undaunted and apparently deaf as well, surged forward. "I can give you twenty dollars plus a brand-new, large family-sized, fully illustrated, gold-leafed, tabbed genuine King James version. What do you say?"

Mr. Angell had been tactfully easing William toward the still-open door. "Mr. Hicken, I do know the true value of that Bible, and I repeat that I will not sell it, nor will I trade it. I suggest that when you get home, you ought to read the one you already have. Sorry to see you leave so soon." So saying, he gently pushed the startled banker through the door.

As William blustered down the walk, fuming all the way to his home, Mr. Angell sat down to record a few more words in his journal. "William is furious and thinks me a fool. I know he will be back, and perhaps he will be even more impudent than his greedy nature made him tonight. It may be time for me to approach the others, to warn them not to sell."

Mr. Angell need not have worried about the others. Their experiences in that world of spirits kept the volumes close to their hearts and locked prudently from sight. Charles was not ready to have Greta come upon the book and toss it out for the second time. He also was not prepared to have her read with him. The moment would have to be right. Lottie decided that her clientele would spread the word all over town, and the experience was too precious to her to be shared with everyone just now. Dory knew she could not yet share her dreams with her aunt either. She had felt Ginny's curious eyes upon her since she related the shadow story a few days ago. Nancy feared that the children would find hers and perhaps read something frightening, such as the Crucifixion or Lazarus rising from the dead.

When William approached each of them, he received negative responses from every one. Charles: "Sorry, William. You couldn't possibly replace this one."

Lottie: "Gee, Mr. Hicken, I'm just not interested in a new one. I like the feel of this one."

Dory: "Mr. C. gave it to me, so it has a lot of sentimental value. You know, he's a great boss."

Nancy: "I just couldn't sell it, Mr. Hicken, seeing it was a gift from the ladies at the church."

When he met next with the tall, opaque, cricket-man, William was troubled but still confident. "I know there are ways to get the books. I've been making plans. Do you need them soon, or can you wait a few days?"

As the man opened his mouth, the pallid and veiled face emitted its rank odor, something similar to the bouquet of old funeral flowers. William knew well enough by now not to stand too close to him. "Unfortunately, I do have a time limit. The sooner you get them to me, the better and more profitable for you. The offer will decrease with the amount of time you take to deliver them. Do not delay, William. See what you can do."

William had already deliberated. He could threaten Nancy Rutledge with foreclosure. He might besmirch Lottie's reputation even more with a few well-dropped remarks in the community. He could promise her that his word was respected. He could offer Dory tremendous opportunity at the bank and lure her away from the bookshop. He might suggest to Charles that a business improvement loan could be had with little or no interest. He knew he must instigate his plans quickly or watch the value of the books decrease daily.

"I can get every one, I promise, but it will take a few days. How do I get in touch with you to let you know? It will be fruitless to meet every day if nothing has happened."

The thin insect-man transferred his weight from one stick leg to the other and stared at William with a penetrating eye. "I will contact you then, if you cannot give me a specific date. But be warned. Every passing day could lower my offer." He turned away from William, as if disgusted by some weakness in the banker. Then he spoke once more. "By the way, if I were you, William, I would not let anyone in your home see the book. Someone might think it useless and throw it away. It's worth too much to you to allow that to happen. Put it aside in a trunk or a drawer until you can deliver them all."

William nodded and headed toward his home. "Good-bye," he called over his shoulder, suddenly eager to be out of the pale man's view.

CHAPTER 29

Another Dreamer

U NDER COVER OF complete darkness, the cricket became immaterial and lay his true murky self across a moldy, lichen-limned gravestone. He resembled an indistinct fog, a meaningless cloud of nighttime mist that one might encounter on the river road. The daytime would dissolve him, as surely as it dispels the fog. In the solitude and grayness of the cemetery, he could now brood and further his plans to eliminate the accursed Bibles. He had chased them across the face of the continent, hounding T. T. Angell and their possessors all the way. It was tiresome that Angell had been able to salvage even these last six. Years had passed, and in spite of the cricket's cleverness, the Bibles still eluded him. Their presence and circulation among people kept him from fulfilling his fate and promise. He was a creature of darkness, literal and spiritual, and dedicated to its promulgation. Angell and the Bibles were in his way. Never being able to maintain a carnate state was a barrier. Never being able to tolerate the light was another. Subterfuge and fright were his only weapons, and they had worked well before. This time, somehow, the task was harder. These people were stubborn and had surely dreamed many dreams. Hicken was his only chance to snag the books before the bookseller came back to Charles and retrieved them. He was gratified to know that Theo was no longer in danger of being under the Bible's influence. Ah, if only more people were as frightened of their dreams as Theo. If only more people were less inclined to believe in anything at all.

Charles decided that same night that it was time to introduce Greta to the wonders of the gold-printed stories in his Bible. After a nice dinner, he helped her in the kitchen and invited her to sit with him by the fire. He asked Greta herself to choose an account from the extraordinary book. "We'll sit right here, next to each other on the divan, and read together. It's been a long time since we did that." Charles was warm and quietly enthusiastic.

"Charles, you know I always have my own private time for reading. But I guess it can't hurt anything. Really, I thought we had gotten rid of that moth-eaten copy."

"Oh, Greta, it's hard for me to explain the exceptional quality of this Bible. The old bookseller said to me that it would make the stories come to life. That's about the best way I can describe what happens after you've read from it." He hesitated to say that others had joined him in that most peculiar adventure. He decided not to tell her about the three readers yet. Greta thumbed through the tissue-thin pages, seemingly disinterested. After a few minutes, she chose one of the parables in the book of Luke, the account of the Good Samaritan. They took turns reading the verses printed in gold. "Charles, it's strange that such a few verses are printed that way. It's a very short story."

"It is, yes, but I'm sure for those who read it there's bound to be special significance."

"Shall we find another in gold ink?"

Charles had never read more than one account at a time. He feared that it would be too much for Greta anyway, and closed the book. Greta took up her knitting basket from the floor and said, "You know, if you had lived back then, you would have been that Samaritan."

He smiled. "Do you really think so? You're probably right. I suppose I would have stopped."

"And I probably would have been home knitting, wondering what was keeping you so long." Greta smiled back at her husband and patted his knee. "I'll fix us some hot cocoa in a while. We'll have it before we go to bed."

Going to bed was exactly what was on Charles's mind. He wondered what Greta would dream and who she would be. It was curious that she had chosen that story and why the next verses were not in gold. He thought she surely would have seen herself in the character of Martha. Tonight would be interesting; tomorrow would tell. Greta was not given to much introspection. In fact, she promptly forgot the significance of her remark about Charles. He *was* the Good Samaritan in town; everyone knew that: an easy mark, a soft touch, and in some ways, a bit of a fool. True, he had never tried to change, not even when Greta berated him for throwing dollars to the wind. "Like so many feathers. You'd think we came by them free in the first place."

"But, Greta," he would say in self-defense, "those people need it more than we do. Surely you can see that." She would always sniff or snort and turn away, leaving him to shake his head at her hard-hearted attitude.

They retired at the usual hour and quickly fell into deep slumber. Charles found himself on a dusty highway, tired, and only half through with the journey from Jerusalem to Jericho. He carried with him spices and fabrics of fine-twined linen and gold threads. It was past high noon. The sun was blazing hot, and he thought to sit in the shadow of some rocks at the side of the highway. He entered the cool shade and felt a sudden blow across his shoulders. He was stunned and fell to the ground. Looking up, he saw four rugged men—highwaymen, bent on thievery and harm.

They pounced upon him, spewing rough language and thumping him with heavy blows. He was defenseless against so many and soon was thrashed into an unconscious state. He lay for a long time, bruised and blistered in the heat of the day. The protecting shadow of the rocks had fled with the sun's journey across the sky. Dark blood dried on the wounds inflicted by the robbers; his ribs and head ached from their punches and kicks. As he lay by the roadside, he heard people pass along. He was helpless to call for aid but aware that several turned aside from him, ignoring his plight. In time, a gently inquiring voice asked of him, "Sir, do you yet live?"

He mustered a nearly inaudible moan but could not move to indicate that he was indeed still living. His eyes were swollen closed, so he could not see the face of his rescuer. The man tended his wounds carefully, washing them with oil and wine, and dressing them. Charles was too weak to utter a word of gratitude but recognized that the stranger had saved his life. After a while, the stranger lifted Charles upon his own beast and carried him to an inn. The innkeeper received some coins and promised to care for Charles until the traveler returned. "He was beaten and robbed along the wayside, and I could not pass him by. I will come this way shortly, and if you spend more than this money for his care, I will repay you."

After he left, the innkeeper observed generously to Charles. "See, you were half dead on the highway, yet a lowly Samaritan stopped to save you. I know of a truth that many of your own kind pass by there daily. Still it was he who stopped to give you aid. You are fortunate, sir."

Even in his dazed condition, Charles had been roused by the voice of that Samaritan. When he awoke in the morning, he realized two things: first, he had not seen Greta in the dream at all, and second, the voice of the Samaritan belonged to Mr. Angell.

Greta's awakening was dramatic. Charles had already arisen by the time she got up from her bed. She could barely hold back her emotion. The dream had been a stark revelation, one that she could not mistake. No wonder Charles wanted to keep the Bible so close. The dream had been as real as the bed she slept in and as warm in her veins as her own lifeblood. It also settled heavily upon her as an unwelcome reprimand. As she dreamed, she found herself in the company of people not mentioned in the scriptures. She was with a group of impious, self-seeking travelers, those who journeyed easily from one city to another, minding no one's needs but their own. They were not without means and protection. They did not suffer, nor did they want for goods or creature comforts. She and her friends had come upon a poor fellow, obviously in need of aid. He had been beaten and, from the looks of him, robbed of nearly everything. "He is surely already dead," observed one of the party. "Leave him. Did you not see that the Levite just ahead of us passed around him? Let us follow the example." Then they all laughed and turned away.

Greta's curiosity had been piqued, and she strained to see the face of the stripped unfortunate. Her shock was absolute as she recognized the man as someone whom she knew well. She hung back a little and saw that a stranger bent over him. Yet she was constrained by convention and society to travel on, leaving behind her own husband to be tended by the mysterious Mr. Angell.

When she awoke, Greta knew that the person she was in her dream was the person she was in her heart. She was ashamed and angry. Ashamed because she saw herself in an unfavorable light. Angry because it was true. She tried to deny the reality of the dream, the stark revelation. She was angry too with Charles. He knew this would happen, she reasoned. He tricked her into reading the verses printed in gold. It was some sort of fraud or deception. She must have only imagined the man to be Charles. But it was so real! She had actually felt the sand grating her soles in her leather sandals, the heat of the day against her face. The beating sun had left its mark on her bare arms. Worse, she knew that she would have passed by the beaten man, avoiding contact and the corruption that had befallen him. At that moment, Charles entered the room.

Greta's icy glare prompted a quizzical look from Charles. "What is it, dear?" he asked, curious. Since he had not seen her in his dream, he had concluded that she had not been there, that somehow she was immune to the powers of the ancient scripture.

She wanted to put him on the defensive and answered his question with two of her own. "Why did you want me to read with you last night, Charles, and what did you think would happen if I read with you?"

"I was merely hoping we could share something, something exciting and rare. A dream, actually."

"Is it rare to dream, Charles? Did you dream last night?"

Now Charles used the same tactic Greta had employed. "Did you?"

She turned away from him and went to the window. The naked limbs of a walnut tree in their yard reached for her and scratched at the glass pane. The sky spread above, the color of pewter, awaiting some burnish from a distant sun. "Was I in your dream, Charles?" she asked, quiet and stony.

"Greta," he said, shaking his head, "you weren't. I was hoping you would be, but no, I didn't see you anywhere."

"If you had seen me, who would I have been?"

"I don't honestly know. There were no women mentioned in the verses. But you chose them, so I thought. . . well, I thought that they would be important ones for you to read. I guess it was just for me."

She stared down into the yard. The grass was dead now, the chrysanthemums stood waiting to be trimmed, and their flowers were browned from the wind and chill of autumn. "You have dreamed like that before? What is it about the dream, Charles? What is it about the gold verses?"

Charles sat at the foot of the bed and folded his hands, letting them fall between his knees. "The old bookseller said they would make the stories come to life. I didn't realize what he meant until I read for myself."

"So what are your dreams like? I'm assuming you've already had a few."

"Yes, I've had several dreams. They're fantastic. It's as if you are there, in person. The first one I had was about the Creation. It was like being there, actually participating. It's been the same every time. And it's not just me. Others have dreamed as well, and we've seen each other in the dreams."

"Oh? You've read with others? How is it you read with other people before you read with me?"

"Well, they have their own Bibles. After we realized the power of the verses, we just agreed on which stories to read. We always see each other in the dreams. I know it sounds fantastic, but it's true. Dory says it's more than dreaming; it really is *being* there!"

"Dory? You've read with *Dory?* She's just a child!" Greta spun about, incredulous. "Who else has been in these dreams?"

Charles decided to open up completely to Greta. He saw hurt enter her eyes, fringing them with beads of salt water. It was irregular to find tears in Greta's eyes, and he saw an insecure show of emotion. "Lottie Mariah is one, Nancy Rutledge is the other. And Dory, of course. There are two more who have Bibles, but we doubt they have even read anything. Bill Hicken has a Bible, and Theo Atwood has one."

Greta could not believe her ears! Lottie Mariah and that Rutledge woman? What was Charles involved in? Suddenly, she remembered someone else she had seen in her dream, someone she did know.

"Does Mr. Angell have one?"

"No, there were just the six I bought. But that is a good question, because I saw him in my dream last night."

"If he doesn't have a Bible, then how did he get there?"

Greta paced her questions. Charles jumped to his feet. "He must have read from one of the books. What made you ask about him?"

"I have a confession to make, Charles. Even if you didn't see me in your dream, I saw you in mine."

"Greta! Then you did dream?"

"Oh, yes, I did." She choked back regret but knew she had to tell him what was on her mind. "And you were in it. You weren't the Good Samaritan, though. Anyone would have thought that you, of all people, would have been him. But in my dream, you were the traveler who was beaten and robbed."

"And Mr. Angell was the Good Samaritan! Yes, yes! We both saw him then. But, Greta, where were you in your dream?"

"I was in a crowd that passed you by, Charles. I saw Mr. Angell stop and help you, and I walked on with my friends. I was afraid and too proud to stop." She put her hands over her eyes and noiselessly wept. Charles went to her and held her in silence. She was ashamed before him yet needed the comfort he offered. After a time, the weeping ceased, and she sniffled like a small child. "Now, I'm afraid to read again. I'm afraid to find out who I might be in another story. I'm afraid of who I really must be, Charles."

She wept fresh tears. Charles wept as well. Though they had traveled separate roads these last few years, they now stood at the beginning of a new path, paved curiously with gold ink.

CHAPTER 30

Commerce

WILLIAM REFUSED TO believe Charles's outlandish tale about a spirit following the Bibles. "Hogwash! Horse puckey! I never heard such trash. I'll bet you believe in the tooth fairy and Santa Claus too! Listen, Charles, I'll buy a whole box of Bibles for your shop if you'll just trade me the old one. How about an interest-free improvement loan? Your wife has been after you for years to update your house."

"How would you know a thing like that?"

"Women. They all talk. Everything gets around. You could make points with her. She'd think you were a shrewd businessman. She'd stop nagging you for this and that and getting upset every time you bought some worthless stuff for your store."

Charles stared at him, incredulous. William retorted quickly. "Like I said, word gets around."

"Well, then, William," replied Charles, "the last worthless stuff I bought seems to have gone up in value, at least in your mind. Maybe it has in her mind too. May I say, unequivocally, that the Bible is not for sale, I do not want an interest-free loan, and it wouldn't hurt you to read the Bible you have before you go trying to make money from it."

William snorted in frustration. "I told you, Charles. I'm *collecting* them."

"And I'm the ghost of Jacob Marley!" Charles laughed, going back to his work.

Rejected and dejected, William made haste to Lottie's shop. She was finishing a comb-out, and he was forced to wait outside, pacing like a tiger at the zoo. He rehearsed his lines over and over during that time and counted the paver stones from the sidewalk to the house as well.

After her client left, William unleashed his fictitious concoction. "Heard the new mortician spent some time at your place a few afternoons ago. Seems a little odd, since you only do women's hair. Seems he was in there a long while too, at least that's what I heard. My wife says she had to wait outside for her regular appointment, and Mr. Angell avoided looking at her when he came out."

"What are you insinuating here? I don't believe your wife would tell a story like that. She was even a little early for her appointment, if you must know!" Lottie Mariah glared in distaste at the banker. "I may not be the Snow Queen, but I certainly never did go after Mr. Angell or any other man in this two-bit town. You high and mighty types are all the same. How about if I go looking through your dirty laundry, eh? What do you want, anyway? You *must* want something."

"All right, so I may have the story a little twisted. But the fact is, with your, you should pardon the expression, reputation, it wouldn't take long to get around town. You'd find yourself curling cat hair for a living if you were lucky. All I want is that Bible you bought from Charles. Once I have it, I promise you—not a word! I'll even pay you more than you gave for it."

"You must really want it in a bad way, Mr. Hoity-toity Big Shot Banker. Well, let me tell you this! It doesn't matter what kind of past I had, I'm a different person now, and nothing you say can hurt me. I know who I am! And I have close friends who know me too. Just get on out of here with your browbeating! You ought to give your Bible back to Charles, so somebody else could read it and get some good out of it. Go peddle your papers somewhere else!"

William backed his way out of Lottie's front door, hoping no one had seen him. She followed hotly after him and shouted as he left, "How in heaven's name did you ever trap that sweet little lady into marrying you? I feel sorry for your whole family!"

He hurried around the corner, supremely annoyed. Lord, these people were obstinate. William's third visit was to Dory's home. Her Aunt Ginny answered the door. She did not recognize him as the banker. On a whim, William approached her about the Bible.

"Oh, yes," she said. "Dory came home with the oddest story about a spirit chasing her on account of having the Bible. But, you know, I think she still has it in her room. And to tell the truth, I do think there's something funny about it. She goes out of here some mornings almost in a daze. I feel sure it's because of reading from it. I saw once that it had gold ink printing."

"Did you read any of it? Was there anything unusual about it, other than the gold ink?"

"Read it? Oh, heavens, no. My eyesight is too poor."

"Well, I am in the way of collecting Bibles of that sort, and you see, it was sold to the bookshop by mistake. Uh, Charles has sent me to collect it and replace it with a new one."

"Well, isn't that nice?"

"So," urged William, anxiously scanning the street, "can you get it for me right now? I will be sending a brand-new one to her in a couple of days. Gold-leafed edges, pictures, the whole package!"

"Well, I could just have a little look. Won't you come in and wait a minute?"

It was like stealing candy from a baby. Too easy but gratifying nonetheless. To soothe his conscience just the slightest, he left five dollars with Aunt Ginny. He doubted Charles had paid that much for the book himself. He returned to the bank and placed the Bible safely in an innocent-looking box in the vault. Next he would see Nancy Rutledge.

As it happened, William knocked on the door of an empty house that afternoon. The children were in school; Nancy was away, cleaning a church lady's house. He had come prepared to lean on her by threatening to foreclose. Now, because the house was unoccupied, another more direct plan entered his schemes. He looked around. The street was remote. No one was about. He jiggled the front doorknob and found that it turned easily. He had no more than to walk into the house, and the book would be his. It took only a few minutes of searching to find the Bible. Nancy had placed it on a high shelf where the children would not likely find it. He located a jar in the cupboard and put five dollars into it—more mollifying of his guilty mind.

William slinked away, self-satisfaction and stealth vibrating in his thin, mean-spirited, and greedy chest. Now he had three of the Bibles—half of the treasure. He had already counted and spent and saved the money promised him a dozen times. How did this really hurt any of these people? They were more than compensated. Bibles were cheap. Print was cheap. The books all said the same thing anyway.

He decided to wait at the bank that evening to see if the man in the cloak would stop by. He felt that having three of the Bibles gave him good leverage for dickering, something of a good-faith show.

The cricket-man did come along, emerging from the shadows silently and odiforously. He seemed to always startle William, but the banker's slight apprehension in the man's presence was overcome by his avarice. However, during each encounter, William braced himself slightly. He was unprepared for the response he would get from the pale visitor this time.

"Three Bibles are unacceptable at this point! I was hoping you would have all, with the possible exception of the one that walking malediction has." The cricket-man rustled somewhere beneath his clothing, like a scarecrow losing moldy straw in the wind. He seemed to shrink with each movement, but his restless behavior continued. The pungency rising out of the man's shifting movements was worse than before. William felt like gagging.

"You may have to steal the Bibles from the other three of them as well." The words were blatant and grated on William's sensibilities.

"I repaid both of those women for the books. I would not refer to it as stealing."

"Of course not. It was rude and insensitive of me to suggest such a thing. What I meant was that you may have to use the same method of commerce with Charles and the hairdresser. The undertaker could be more difficult. His kind always is."

"You seem to have some personal gripe against Mr. Angell. Do you know him from somewhere else?"

"I have known him practically my whole life." The cricket-man's words came like the hiss of a snake in tall, dry grass, stale and strangely menacing. "I will give you another twenty-four hours before the offer is reduced. I trust you will not let me down, William." So saying, he swept away, brittle and practically dissected by the time he rounded the corner. His corporeal shape gave way to the gray mass that he really was, the disembodiment of darkness. He was off to brood in the cemetery once more, hoping that William's heart was full of enough covetousness that he could finally remove all of the Bibles from circulation.

CHAPTER 31

Other Forces at Work

NANCY WAS DEVASTATED to find her Bible missing. She did not connect the mysterious five dollars with the disappearance of the scriptures until she spoke with Dory at the bookshop. They had both run to Charles immediately upon their discoveries.

"My aunt says it was a nice young man, a collector who was going to send me a brand-new Bible. She said he told her Charles had sent him. She figured I would rather have a new one anyway and let him have the Bible. He left five dollars too."

Dory was near tears and angry. Nancy shook her head. "I can't believe someone would just walk right into my house and steal it like that. He has to be the same person who left the money with your aunt. Who do we know who would go that far to collect books? He must know about the gold printing and the dreams."

"I think that's one problem. He *doesn't* know about the dreams."

"He must not know about the shadowy thing either. Mr. C., who do you think it is?"

Charles realized he must tell them, now that things had gone this far. "I'm certain it's Bill Hicken, the banker. He was here earlier, trying to finagle a deal with me. Offered me an interest-free loan, just to get his hands on the Bible. He used the same collector lie with me as with your aunt. He must have a terrific offer to go to such lengths. We'll have to see Lottie and ask about her Bible. She and I and Theo have the remaining three books."

Charles then recalled that Mr. Angell had been in his dream. "I wonder, did either of you let the new undertaker read from your Bibles?" Their response was negative. Charles was all the more confused then and decided to go immediately to Lottie and ask her a few questions. "Dory, I'll be gone about an hour. The shop is all yours until I get back."

Charles hurried through the November afternoon, fortified against the wind by his old wool jacket. Lottie was just combing out her last clients of the day, the Anderson sisters, and they were discussing Nancy's progress.

"She's doing well. The ladies in the circle are so pleased with her work, and her children seem ever so much freer. It's a blessing that good has come of her tragedy."

"Well, aren't you ladies a big part of that good?"

Lottie referred to their efforts in teaching Nancy to read. She went on. "Oh, she already told me about not being able to read. You're helping her a lot, you know. And I have to say that I thought for a long time you two were like all those other women at the church, you know, just interested in looking good and not really being good. Not that I'm any great shakes at it myself."

The sisters raised four eyebrows and exchanged glances. "Ahem," said Ardis, "we think you are probably better than you realize, Lottie." Suddenly, they were aware of Charles standing in the doorway. He was fiddling with his hat, turning it around and around in his hands.

"Oh, Mr. C.," said Lottie, adopting Dory's nickname for Charles. "We're almost finished here." The Andersons, who were on their way out, exchanged pleasantries with Charles and left. "What's up?" asked Lottie, sensing that something was amiss.

"Did Bill Hicken come here today, trying to get your Bible?"

"Did he ever! What a worm! He threatened to spread rumors about me and Mr. Angell if I didn't turn the book over to him. Can you believe it? Of course, he offered me money too. I nixed the whole idea, though, and told him to go peddle his papers someplace else. Why? Is he bothering you with that stuff too?"

"Oh, yes, although he used a different ploy with me. That's not all. He wangled Dory's away from her aunt and apparently walked right into Nancy's empty house and took hers. In each case, he left five dollars."

"That still sounds like stealing to me! And what's it called, what he said to me?"

"*Extortion* is the word that comes to mind in your case."

"What's with him, anyway?"

"I think he has a buyer lined up, someone who has offered him a lot of money. Hang onto that book for your life, Lottie! Hide it somewhere and don't tell a soul where it is, except perhaps one of us. I'm going over to Theo's and see if Bill tried to get his."

"That old Bible?" Theo's frightening episode came back suddenly to haunt him. He had managed to stuff it away in the last couple of days, but now here it was again. "Aw, I figured it was an eyesore in here, so I foisted it off on Mr. Resurrection himself. He's always preachin' that kind of stuff."

"Mr. Resurrection?" Theo could only mean one person by that remark.

"Oh, I see. You gave it to Mr. Angell?" Charles was beginning to see why Angell had showed up in his and Greta's dream.

"That's the one. I'm getting me a new model, nice and neat looking, to put out for the bereaved. That is, if anybody else ever shows up to be buried here. The old meat wagon is getting rusty out back."

Charles winced at Theo's euphemism for the ancient hearse in his garage. He sensed an edge in Theo's voice and tried to lay it on the lack of business lately. Still, Theo seemed inordinately relieved to be rid of the Bible. Perhaps he had read and dreamed after all. Perhaps, like Greta, he had seen someone he did not like in his scriptural flight.

"Tell me, did Bill Hicken ever approach you about buying the Bible?"

"Yeah, sure he did. Said he could probably turn a profit on it if it was old enough. Or else he's collecting them. Of course, I never knew him to collect anything but mortgages myself. I didn't sell it to him, though, just on general principles. At any rate, if you want it back yourself, you'll have to see the wingless wonder over there." Theo dismissed Charles immediately by turning his back and whistling tunelessly into the musty, static, and funereal air.

T. T. Angell was not in when Charles knocked at the mortuary door across town. He tried the back entrance to the owner's quarters, but no one answered there either. It was frustrating since he felt that Mr. Angell, once he knew about Bill's plans, would be a strong ally in saving the Bibles. As Charles rounded the corner of the building, the mortician himself came toward him. The man smiled, revealing the golden-capped tooth. "Ah, Charles, to what do I owe this welcome visit?"

"Hello, Mr. Angell. I need to talk with you about the Bible that belonged to Theo Atwood. Do you still have it? Has anyone tried to buy it from you?"

Mr. Angell unlocked his door and invited Charles to enter his living room. It was sedate and simply furnished. Mr. Angell walked directly to a small bookcase and withdrew the ancient scriptures. "It's right here, Charles. And yes, someone did try to buy it. Mr. Hicken from the bank inquired about it, but as you see, he was not successful."

"Thank heaven!" exclaimed Charles.

"Indeed," added Mr. Angell.

"As you might guess, there is something very special about these Bibles. But I'm wondering if you don't already know that. It was pointed out to me by the bookseller who left them a few days ago. I don't suppose you've run into this kind of thing before?"

"Do you refer to the gold printing on some of the verses?"

"Yes," said Charles. "The gold printing and something else."

Mr. Angell rubbed his long fingers across the book cover, caressing it gently and lovingly. He did not immediately respond to Charles. A peaceful silence pervaded the room, and the very air seemed pure, like the crystal breath of a mountain stream. Then Mr. Angell spoke. "You speak of the dreams, do you not?"

Then he *had* read! Charles was certain of it. "Yes, yes! I knew you must have read. You were right there. You saved my life on the road to Jericho. Were you surprised? Wasn't it wonderful? There are others of us who dream, you know. Lottie Mariah, Dory, Nancy Rutledge. Even my wife dreamed last night after she read with me. Did you see her there?" His words were coming in a heated rush. He thought he must have sounded silly. "Oh, I'm chirping on, just like Dory. Of course, it would be hard to believe that anyone was *really* there, wouldn't it?"

Charles had hardly been this electrified about the dreams with anyone. Maybe it was because Mr. Angell was another man; maybe it was because he was on the verge of accepting the dreams as events in place, rather than strong visions. Whatever the reason, he felt Mr. Angell would share in the enthusiasm and urgency of the situation. He continued speaking. "We can't let Bill get any more of the Bibles, and we should definitely try to get the others back, before he sells them off. What do you think we should do?"

"First of all, how many do you say he has?"

"He has his own, Dory's, and Nancy's. I refused to let him even see mine, Lottie's is safe, and the last is yours."

"How did he get Dory's and Nancy's?"

"He as good as stole them, that's how. At any rate, we have to find a way to get them back."

"Stole them? He must want them very badly. Let me think for a while on the problem. Perhaps I can speak with Mr. Hicken myself and get a clear view of what is happening."

"That's great!" said Charles, relieved to be sharing his burden with another male. "Call me as soon as you talk to him." He paused before leaving, contemplating the marvel of the dreams once again. "Why do you suppose the dreams are possible, Mr. Angell? I have a feeling you are not surprised by them."

"Let's only say that I have experienced this sort of thing before. Explanations are rather difficult, but I can say that you and the others are only a few of the very fortunate. You are right to be concerned about the selling of the Bibles. We have to prevent them from falling into the wrong hands."

Charles left Mr. Angell intending to go straight to the shop. His mind was cluttered with a jumble of facts and some quizzical impressions. Mr. Angell obviously knew much about the Bibles, obviously had dreamed himself. His awareness of their importance and eagerness to protect them from Hicken was also evident. He had an air about him of timeless wisdom, extensive consciousness, calmness, and surety. And his fleeting resemblance, even in spirit, to the old seller of books, how could that be explained? There was more at work here, Charles reasoned, than magic books and potent dreams. He arrived at his shop in a muddled daze, unable as yet to connect the pieces of this priceless puzzle. Opening the door, he found Dory and Greta conversing in distraught tones.

"Charles!" Greta cried. "I had no idea! He said you had

sent him! He told me the book was going into your safe deposit box."

Charles raised his hands to calm his confessing wife. "Who? What are you talking about?"

"It was a clerk from the bank. Mr. Hicken must have sent him over to your house with that lie so he could get the Bible." Dory continued the narrative. "Mrs. C. believed him and gave it to the clerk."

"Good heavens! How does he think he can get away with this?" Charles was dumbfounded. "Now he has all but two of them."

"I'm so sorry, Charles. I just didn't know. And I thought, since the book seemed to have such power, that you would naturally want to keep it safe."

"It was stupid of me not to mention that Bill was after it. I never imagined he would stoop to such tricks. It's not your fault, Greta. We'll find a way to get it back."

While Charles and the dreamers were searching for an answer to the problem of Bill Hicken, other forces were at work devising a way to get the last two copies of the Bible. It was dusk, and the cricket-man had assembled himself. He was now able to muster enough strength at the end of each day to materialize for longer periods of time.

He intended to go first to Lottie's. Writing a note required a huge effort on his part; physical acts were not a part of his natural makeup. It had taken many years to perfect the art of materializing at all, and the ability to actually touch the physical world was often fleeting. He carefully applied a pen to an old slip of yellowed note paper. The note was simple: *Lottie, you must bring the Bible to the bookshop right away, Dory.*

He slipped through the darkness to Lottie's home and located the phone line running up the brick wall. The line was cut with the rasping of his long, sharp nails, and then he placed the note under her doormat. He immediately rapped loudly at her door, slipped around the house, and waited. The porch light flicked on, and Lottie came to the door, peering into the night. "Who's there?" she called. "Halloween's over, you know. Wiseacre!" Then she saw the note protruding from beneath the doormat and reached down to get it. When she rose up, she sniffed the air in disgust. "What in the world is that? Smells like a dead skunk! Yech!"

She read the note quickly and retreated into the house. Her first reaction was to phone Charles at the shop. The line was dead. Perhaps that's why the note was sent. She wondered why Dory had not waited for an answer, but she remembered the girl's stories about being spooked. It was silliness as far as she was concerned. She thought for another moment and then went to the bedroom to retrieve the wondrous Bible from its hiding place. *Charles must have a plan,* she thought, throwing on her coat and scarf. She placed the Bible in a mesh shopping bag and dropped her house key into the coat pocket. Leaving a light burning in the parlor and one on the porch, she left the house.

It was one of those evenings that was so quiet you could hear cats whispering through pickets. The bustle of day was deliciously suspended. This autumn had stubbornly held on to some of November, so that occasional vestiges of gentle haze lay upon the sunset, lingering through the twilight into nighttime. Tonight was such a night. Lottie stepped smartly off her porch, listening to the sound of her own footfalls on the paved walk. At once, she was acutely aware of that same fetid odor she had noticed at her doorstep. She stopped suddenly and turned, just in time to stand face-to-face with the opaque and repulsively gaunt cricket-man. Her first instinct was to scream, which she did. Her second was not to be silenced by fear. Instead, she spit out a brilliant and indefinably virgin string of epithets, aimed in the direction of the reeking haunt. Accompanying the magnificent verbal brass was a barrage of strikes at the shocked cricket-man. She laid into him with the mesh bag and the old Bible acted as a sort of holy ballast.

In his fleshly state, the cricket-man had never before

encountered combat. His greatest weapons had been intimidation and various lures. Lottie was a new phenomenon. The energies needed to maintain his worldly form were expended quickly in self-defense. Before Lottie's eyes, he melted from the cloaked figure, dissolving to arrange himself once more to the gray mass that had frightened Dory. Lottie knew immediately that this was what Dory had seen. She stood her ground and protested to the pulsing cloud. "You can't get *my* Bible, you perverted pile of waste!" She ran straight to the porch, where the light still burned brightly. She went into the house and rummaged in a kitchen drawer to locate a flashlight, all the while talking and blasting the thing outside. "If I can't call Charles and figure this thing out, then you'll just have to fly behind, because I'm taking the light with me!"

At the bookshop, Charles sat impatiently wondering why he was not able to make a telephone connection with Lottie. "I can't get her. Something is wrong, because the telephone doesn't even ring. I'd better get over there and find out what's happening." He had no sooner opened the bookshop door than he saw Lottie running toward him, waving a flashlight in all directions as she hurried.

"Mr. C.! Mr. C. Do you see him? Is he behind me?" she called to Charles, breathless. She ran past him and collapsed on a bench by the counter. Her breathing was ragged, and in spite of the cool night, perspiration drenched her forehead. She clutched the Bible tightly to her bosom as relief washed over her. "Do you see him anywhere?"

"Lottie!" blurted Greta. "You look as if you had just seen a ghost!"

William was pacing nervously by the time the reconstructed cricket appeared in front of the bank. The street was deserted, and the barest ray of light reached out to the doorway. Still, even in the dimness, the translucence of the mysterious buyer was evident. He was worn thinner by his efforts to get Lottie's Bible. "I have four of the Bibles now," William spoke positively in the direction of the cloaked man. "I'm certain that by tomorrow evening I will have them all. What do you say to sticking with the original offer? You know how difficult these people can be."

Stick-man shivered and blew dust from his nostrils in agreement. "Yes, I certainly do. I am trying to be understanding, William, believe me. All right, but after tomorrow night I shall have to lower my offer."

"You wouldn't consider taking the four now and the other two tomorrow?"

"Perhaps, but it is unlikely I can give you the full amount. I'll have to see."

"Are you just an agent then, for someone else? I was under the impression you were on your own. Do I have the wrong information?"

"Almost all information is based on impression, William. We take what we see and make our own truth out of it. What does it matter to you who the books finally go to? Do you want the money or not?"

"The money, yes."

"Tell me, William, where do you keep the books you have now?"

"They are in the bank vault. They're completely safe. No one else even knows what they are or what they're worth."

"You are mistaken, William. Our friend, the new mortician, knows their worth. You will have to be very canny with him. And that Lottie person. She is unpredictable to say the least."

"How do you know these people anyway? You're a stranger here."

"Here? This place is just like any other. I've seen the likes of all of you a thousand times. You each look different, and some of you have more goods than the rest, but basically you are the same. I'm afraid that as a race, you people are simple and often pretentious. You think you know so much, but in reality, you are backward and pitifully unsophisticated, present company excluded, of course."

"That would be both of us, I gather," said William, irritated.

"Oh, indeed. Well now, to the business at hand. Perhaps I could just take the four Bibles you have in your safe and then come back for the last two tomorrow. Why don't you go and get them right now?"

"Not without the money!" insisted the banker. "Show me that share of the money first." The cricket-man was growing impatient and fatigued. He had spent far too much time in his embodied state, and it was fast wearing him thin. He knew he did not have sufficient duration for the transaction if he had to materialize money as well. He would have to put William off with some excuse.

"I've left it at my place. I guess I can wait until tomorrow. I will bring the whole amount then."

Then William was distracted by a noise in the street, and when he turned to resume his conversation, the insect-man was gone. What had the man meant when he referred to "you people as a race"?

CHAPTER 32

Going for Theo

T HE READERS WHO were now gathered at the bookshop decided to go in a body to Nancy's house and then to the mortician. They hoped that together they might advance some plan to retrieve the books. They carefully hid Lottie's Bible and marched into the night, finding strength in numbers.

Nancy was just ending a reading session with Ardis and Adele when Charles knocked. The women were surprised to see such an entourage appear at Nancy's doorstep. Obviously, they were not merely out for an evening stroll. Charles looked rather sheepish now, standing there with his three females in tow. They all seemed to look to him for instruction. After an awkward moment, Lottie spoke up. "Ladies, I wonder if you wouldn't mind staying with the kids for about an hour. We, uh, sort of have a treat for Nancy. You know, a surprise?" The sisters glanced at Nancy, as if awaiting approval. Nancy nodded and asked, "If you could?"

Scurrying along like a gaggle of hushed geese, they spoke in whispered tones. "I take it the sisters don't know about the Bibles," said Charles.

"No, not yet," Nancy replied. "I didn't know if there would ever be a good time to tell them. And now, since mine is gone—"

"Through no one's fault, mine is gone too, Nancy. That means the only Bibles William doesn't have are Lottie's and Mr. Angell's. We want to go to his place and have all of us decide what to do."

Arriving quickly, they were ushered inside the undertaker's living quarters. "We definitely have a problem," Charles began. "This time the thing was bolder. It came to Lottie's door, somehow wrote a note, and tricked her into going outside with the Bible."

"I remembered the bit about the light, how it couldn't stand the light, so I got my flashlight and beat it for Mr. C.'s shop," Lottie reported. "Wait! I forgot the part about how he looked like a man. He was dressed up in old-fashioned clothes, though. And the stink!"

"We need a plan to get the Bibles back from Mr. Hicken," said Dory, "before anything worse happens."

"Does anyone know where the Bibles are kept?" Mr. Angell asked.

"Do we?" Lottie glanced from person to person.

"I think that he would keep them in a safe place," said Greta, who had said little to this point. "You know, a *safe* place?" She was still churning inside from letting the Bible go on such a thin pretense. The significance of the ancient scriptures had sunk deeply into her mind, and her sudden introspection continued to stir profound feelings. While the others questioned and posed various answers, she had turned her thoughts over and over in silence.

"Charles!" she said abruptly. "I have another confession to make. I have money in the bank I've never mentioned to you. It came to me when my mother died. I was afraid to let you know about it, so I put it in a safe deposit box, and it's been there ever since."

"Afraid?" questioned Charles. "Why were you afraid?"

"Well, you know how generous you are with money. I was afraid that you'd wind up giving it to every down-and-outer who came along."

"But, Greta, not if it was your money!" Charles was incredulous.

"Oh, Charles, I see that now. Maybe I was being selfish as well. I thought if I had any investments I might lose money on those too, so I just kept it there."

"So, what are you saying here, Mrs. C.?" Lottie asked.

"What I'm saying is that if Bill Hicken has the Bibles in the safe in his bank, I may be able to use the pretense of visiting my money to find them. Or offer him what I have in there."

Charles was astounded. "Buy them?" Mr. Angell smiled behind his upraised hand. *Greta is going to be all right after all,* he thought. There was a rush of 'oohs' from the other women. Greta had unwittingly made three new friends.

The mortician spoke. "I have a feeling we would not be able to match any sum that has been offered him already. Just think. He has stooped to thievery and deceit to get them away from us. The offer must be very . . ."

"Huge!" Lottie exclaimed.

"Mammoth!" whispered Dory, thinking of the paltry sum Charles paid for them. "I wonder if the bookseller knew what he was carrying around in that beat-up old box."

"Secret treasure," sighed Charles.

"I have an idea. I can go to William and demand to see the Bible. I'll tell him I left something of sentimental value in the Old Testament. That way I can find out if he has them at the bank." Greta had not ceased scheming.

"You should call him too!" Lottie looked at Dory and Nancy. "You should back him into a corner, make him confess, and just return your Bibles. Or here's another idea. What if I call him and tell him I'm willing to sell, for the right price."

"Or we could all face him." It seemed everyone had an opinion except Mr. Angell. Charles turned to look at him and continued. "What do you think?"

T. T. Angell had been watching the little group carefully to determine how far they might be willing to go to retrieve the Bibles. Sometimes drastic measures were required to save the Word, and he felt that now was just such a time. In his position as guardian of the books, he could not interfere once people possessed them. It would be up to the readers themselves to save the Bibles. He chose his next words with prudence. "I think that you are going to have to enlist the help of Theo Atwood."

All eyes stared in disbelief. Theo had given his copy away! He had not even read. He was a complete heretic. Why would they need Theo's help? Their skeptical expressions begged the question, why?

"The answer is complicated but simple. Theo *has* read, and he has *dreamed,* mark my words. The reason he so willingly let his copy go is that what he read frightened him. He attributed his dream and his fright to hocus-pocus and voodoo. He obviously read something none of us read at the same time. If he can be convinced to read with the group and, therefore, dream with the group, we will have him on our side. Theo is the answer."

"But how can we do that? His mind has always been set against religion and anything to do with it. He thinks it's absurd superstition. We've all heard him try to humiliate Reverend Gillette and anybody else who believes." Charles spoke out of confusion. He was not understanding Mr. Angell's point.

"Try to recall what the bookseller told you. That might give you a clue."

"Well, he said that when you read the gold ink passages, they come to life. He said that the books would be worth much more than I paid for them, and, let's see, oh yes, he said there were people in my little town who desperately needed these books."

"He was right about that!" said Lottie. "I was one of those people."

"And so was I," said Nancy quietly.

"We all must have needed the Bibles," Dory added. "But, Mr. C., I don't see why you would need one. You're already, well, you know, good."

"Oh, come now. I'm no better than the rest of you. It's not that we aren't already good," said Charles. "We all are. I see it as this. We are all lacking certain qualities that will add to our happiness and usefulness. The stories have made us aware of those things."

Dory spoke. "And they have let us know that we can overcome our old selves. I used to think I was a nothing. I had no parents, and nobody thought I was anything special, but Mr. C. gave me the chance to use my drawing, and my posters brought attention to the Bibles. I really felt like I had a lot to do with selling them because of that."

"The first words I ever read well at all were some of the verses in my Bible," added Nancy. "I picked it up, and, like magic, I was able to understand the whole story. That helped me make friends with the Anderson sisters, and now they're teaching me to read for myself."

"Well, everybody here knows what the town has thought of me," said Lottie. "But I was still like you, Dory. I thought I would never be anybody much. I guess that's why I get mouthy and talk big. I really felt lower than other people. But when I read that first story, and I heard—" Lottie's voice broke, and her lip trembled. She recalled vividly the quiet man's face and gentle manner. Softly, she continued. "When I heard him speak to me, it went right to my heart, you know?" She was unable to proceed and turned her head aside.

Greta sat gravely through these accounts and pondered whether she ought to share her thoughts. There was a short silence following Lottie's comments, and then Greta told her story. "The story I read showed me something I really did not want to know. It showed me what a hypocrite I've been all these years. We read the parable of the Good Samaritan," she explained. "Mr. Angell here was the one who stopped and helped the man on the road. I was with a group of people who passed him by. It felt all right too, in my dream, until I saw who the man was."

All eyes were on her. Charles watched, not with gloating but with pity and understanding. "The beaten man was my own husband, Charles. When I woke up the next morning, I realized that the woman I was in that dream was the woman I am in real life." Charles took her hand and patted it gently. The inner pain she felt filled Mr. Angell's small living room. There was a moment of silence, and then Dory spoke. "I wonder what Theo might have dreamed."

"There's no way of knowing unless we ask him," Charles said and reached for his overcoat. Everyone in the little covey of readers except Mr. Angell donned warm coats and jackets and went to the door.

"Theo does not think much of me at this point," Mr. Angell said. "And my presence might hinder his acceptance of the challenge to read. Why don't you call me after you've seen him?" He pulled his Bible from the shelf and handed it to Charles. "Take this with you, so Theo can read again. If he will read, the right story will come to your minds and you can all read together."

"What about the phantom-thing that follows the Bibles?" asked Nancy, worried.

"I've got my flashlight," said Lottie. "That'll keep it away."

"I think that your numbers will help also. If there's another thing it seems not to like, it's a whole congregation of believers."

"Good enough," agreed Charles. "Let's go!" He and the others were gone in a moment. They arrived without incident at Theo's home. The five of them waited impatiently for the undertaker to answer the door. When he did, he was dressed in a silken smoking jacket, sucking on one of his best see-gars.

His head was clouded in a billow of smoke.

"Trick or treating a little late this year, ain't we?" He looked at them with cynical humor glinting in his eye. "What's up with you and your harem, Charles?"

"We need your help, Theo. May we come in out of the cold?" Theo rarely had visitors. His home was a bachelor's dream, a homemaker's nightmare, and his Shangri-la of personal comfort. He reluctantly allowed them to pass. "One of you planning to buy the farm sometime soon?"

There was no laughter, not even a smile in response to his purposely feeble joke. "We've come about the Bibles," Charles said.

Theo's guard seemed to go up immediately. "You mean the beat-up old books that were in your bookstore? Got rid of mine a day or so ago. I mean to buy a new one. That one was too flimsy for people to handle."

"Maybe it was too hot for *you* to handle," Lottie interjected in her brash way. "We think you know what happens when you read the gold ink verses. We've all read them, and we've all dreamed the stories afterward."

"If you think I'm impressed by the voodoo or spell or whatever it is, then you have another thing coming," Theo answered defensively. Now Charles was sure that Mr. Angell was right. Theo must have dreamed something out of his understanding, something very strong indeed.

"It's not voodoo, Mr. Atwood," added Nancy. "But there is magic about them. I've never been able to read anything much in my whole life, but when I picked up that Bible in the bookstore, I could read the gold stories right away. I could understand every word."

"Theo," Greta injected her assertion, "it's of the utmost importance that we get those Bibles back. You've got to help us!"

"Well, just hop on over to the Angell man for mine then. I gave it to him. What happened to yours anyway? I assume you all had one."

Speaking for the entire group, Charles related the story to Theo, emphasizing Bill Hicken's part in their disappearance. He did not yet include the information about the shade that followed the books. Theo was skeptical and still refused to admit to dreaming. "So what can I do about all this? I don't even have the Bible anymore. Though I would hate to see Hicken make a killing at your expense."

Dory screwed up her courage. "We think that the Bibles were meant to go to certain people in town. Because you bought that first one, you were one of those it was meant for. You should read with us and go with us."

"Go? Go where?"

"To the place we read about," said Charles. "As I explained before, we've seen each other in the stories. We see who we are and who we might become. It's not voodoo, Theo, it's revelation."

"So what do I get out of all this, assuming I do read?"

"Look, we can't promise you anything you don't want to get out of it yourself. The dreams are there for all of us. What we do with them afterward is our own business." Lottie was becoming restless with his reluctance. Theo's memory of his startling dream reminded him that what they said was absolutely true. His experience with the dream could not have been closer to reality. Finding that he would have been one of the Roman soldiers at the foot of the cross had shocked even him. He had felt sick inside ever since the nightmare.

"I'm going tomorrow to find out where Bill is keeping the other books. Meantime, we still have Lottie's and yours. We have to come up with a plan right away before he sells the rest of them."

"Oh, my soul!" declared Greta. "What if he has already sold them?"

"I rather doubt it," said Charles. "I think he has a deal going for all six, since he's trying so hard to get the whole group."

"How do you know Bill hasn't read anything? Maybe

that's why he wants all of them for himself." Theo's question was a good one. He seemed to be pondering the same unanswered questions that the group had addressed earlier. Charles was encouraged. "So, will you read with us?"

CHAPTER 33

Discovering the Books

THEO WAS THE center of attention again, something he
rather liked, surprisingly for an apparent loner. Five pairs
of eyes silently appealed to him, and breathing ceased in
anticipation. The room was as still as a rising moon, as quiet
as Christmas eve at midnight.

"Oh, what the hell!" Theo exploded. "Why not?"

The group decided to allow Theo the privilege of choosing verses from the very Bible he had given Mr. Angell. He
knew nothing of how to select but let the pages fall open
by themselves. The leaves came to rest at St. John, chapter
nine, the story of the man who was blind from birth. The
highlighted passage stopped at verse sixteen. They each read
a verse in turn, and when they finished, they agreed to leave
the book at Theo's since it was rightly his anyway.

It was a strange and wonderful impression Theo had of
his small-town neighbors when he awoke. It was a strange
and equally wonderful feeling he had about life. No one was

surprised that, as they dreamed together, Theo was the blind man. Not even Theo was surprised. It was fitting, it was natural, it was right; this was his revelation, after all.

The others were happy bystanders, already touched by the spirit and presence of the gentle man who healed those who were willing to be healed. Not one among them was in the group of disapproving Pharisees. By now, their dream-travels ran a spontaneous course, and they had come to accept the fantastic occurrences as fundamental, albeit no less thrilling. Though Theo was still a fairly new passenger on this spiritual bubble, he knew the moment he awoke that it must be he who retrieved the Bibles. He was already working out a plan. He was engrossed in his experience and the marvel of it when he heard an early-morning knock at the door. It was Lottie.

"Listen," she said, thrusting herself into the entryway. "I have an idea to get this thing off the ground right away. I want to know what you think of it." She slammed the door closed and launched her plan to a highly interested mortician. It was all of seven o'clock in the morning.

Promptly at nine-thirty, Albert, the mailman, opened the bank doors for his first delivery, and Lottie swept in behind him. She carried with her a brown-paper package. It contained her Bible. She had taken it home the night before from Charles's shop, brandishing her flashlight all the way. Greta and Charles had insisted on accompanying her, and the three arrived safely and saw the Bible safeguarded inside.

After they left, Lottie marched down to her basement and spent the better part of the next hour scouring her many storage boxes. At last, she came up with the objects of her search, went upstairs, and slept like a baby—a dreaming baby, of course. Now she was standing in front of William's office, awaiting his arrival, carrying an oversized bag at her side. When William walked in, she spoke directly to him. "Mr. Hicken, I have a matter of great importance to speak to you about. Let's go in your office." Before he could work up a protest, she hustled him inside and closed the door. She immediately unwrapped the package and laid the Bible on the desk in front of him. "There's the Bible you are so interested in. You can have it for fifty bucks, not a penny less. But let me tell you, there's some kind of curse on it, and for that reason, I'm letting you buy it."

"Why would I want a Bible with a curse on it, pray tell?" He replied to her in his prissiest manner, but his innermost belly was leaping with excitement. Fifty dollars was peanuts compared to what he would get from the cricket-man.

"Because I figure you are going to unload it for a lot more once it's yours. I know about how you got Nancy's and Dory's, but that's no skin off my nose. The thing is, there's some kind of, I don't know how to say it, but some kind of evil that follows it. I'm sick of worrying about it anymore. Like I said, fifty bucks and it's yours."

William reached for his wallet and drew out the amount. He handed it to Lottie and grasped for the Bible. Lottie held back the slightest moment before letting it go. "There is one thing. When I heard about Charles's Bible, he said he left a sentimental sort of bookmark in his. I thought I'd pick it up for him while I'm here." Anxious to be rid of her, William grabbed the book and quickly said, "Well, all right then, I'll go have a look. I'll be right back."

As he left the room, she watched him scuttle through the bank to the vault door. He clutched her precious Bible to himself in greed. It pained her to see him take it, but it was an important part of her plan. She was gratified to see that Greta had guessed on the button. The books were in the bank, all right. It would make the rest of the plan go forward easily. She craned her neck in a successful effort to see him pull a box from the vault. He placed it on a small desk by the vault door and rummaged through the pages of all the Bibles. He finished, looking irritated, and replaced the box on an empty shelf. When he returned, William wore a look of frustration.

"Charles must have been wrong. There was no special bookmark in any of them. It's probably on the floor of his den or something. Now if you'll excuse me, I have important documents to sign."

"Oh, I'm sure you do. Say, you sure this money isn't counterfeit? Looks pretty new to me." She couldn't resist a small chide. William simply stared icily at her and then turned his back. "Good day, Miss Mariah," he answered crisply.

CHAPTER 34

Recovering the Books

LOTTIE'S HEELS CLICKED against the marble flooring as she left the bank. Her next stop was Theo's mortuary. "They're in a plain box on a shelf in the bank vault. Five of the prettiest old books you'll ever see. I'm sure he will go after the last one now he's so close."

"He probably thinks that Angell still has it too. All right. If we can get Angell to call and invite Bill over there to pick it up, then we're home free." Theo was slightly on edge. When Lottie had approached him with her plan at the unearthly hour of seven in the morning, his adrenaline began pumping furiously. It had not stopped since.

"Okay," she said. "I'm on my way to his place right now. As soon as I know Hicken is on his way to Mr. Angell's, I'll let you know."

William was shocked to hear from Mr. Angell. "I've decided to let the Bible go," said the second mortician. "I can see how important this must be to you, the collection and all. I can always buy another one. Could you come over right away? I have business to attend to in Clairesville, and I can't take time to stop at the bank. How much? Oh, I should say twenty dollars would be sufficient. That would buy a nice replacement. Right away then?"

William hung up the telephone, shaking. What luck! What absolute luck! He fled from the bank like a man on fire. As he rounded the corner out of sight, a dark figure walked boldly into the bank. He wore a black hat, black mask, black coat, and black pants. He even sported black gloves and shoes. He carried a big black bag, looking like a Halloween Santa. He pointed something at the people in the bank; they couldn't be sure what because it was concealed by a black scarf. The bank employees stared at one another in complete amazement. Was this an actual robbery? The bank had never been robbed before, unless you could count the many pens that seemed to walk out on a regular basis with patrons.

By the time the man in black said, "Put up your hands," all arms were already in the air. With one gesture of his head and a single word, they fell to the floor, face down. It was as if the scene had been rehearsed a dozen times. In a gruff voice, he ordered the oldest clerk in the room to open the vault and be quick about it. The clerk, who was a lifelong resident of the town, mumbled to himself, "Theo?" and obeyed without delay. The man in black told them to close their eyes and remain on the floor. All of them conformed. *What an obedient bunch,* he thought. *Bill had them trained right.*

He made an act of shuffling through papers and fiddling with combinations, and then he yelled at them, changing his voice again. "Don't dare call the sheriff, and don't anybody breathe a word of this until tomorrow. We have people watching all of your families. If Hicken hears of it, they're dead!" As quickly as he had come, the man in black raced through the front doors and was gone. When the employees checked the vault, it seemed that nothing was missing except their dignity. They had been robbed of a robbery. All the money was still there. All the papers were there. That box of old books was still there. Nothing was missing but the crime.

William returned in his own private funk. Angell had tricked him or already left, for there was no answer to his knock at the mortician's home. He was furious, and vowed to keep trying to reach the man if it took all day. He barked at the employees the minute his shoes hit the marble floor. He was ruder than usual and meaner than ever. Keeping the semi-exciting news from such as Mr. Hicken was not difficult for any of the clerks or officers now. The unspoken consensus was that it was too bad the would-be robber could not have taken good old William hostage.

Lottie and Theo stood proudly in Charles's bookshop. Greta, who was just on her way to the bank to check out her theory, marveled at the speed and success accomplished by the hairdresser and the mortician. Charles dabbed at his moist eyes with a white handkerchief.

"They're all there!" boasted Theo. "I put mine in the box too. Nobody got hurt, nobody recognized me, and when Bill finds out, he'll be puckered for a month."

"Yeah," laughed Lottie. "But what can he say? Somebody robbed him of stuff that he robbed in the first place? It's too sweet."

"So where did you get old Bibles to put in the vault?" Greta was still standing in awe.

"I remembered my grandmother had some things stored in the basement. It seemed to me that she had Bibles all over her place when I was a kid. I always thought that's what drove my dad to drink. Anyhow, I found them and just went through them with a little metallic nail polish here and there. I don't think Billy-boy ever intended to read from them anyway. I'm hoping that if he flips through the pages, he won't notice the difference."

"So, you even got the one Bill bought from me?" Charles asked.

"Every last one, Mr. C.," nodded Lottie. "All six are here.

Now what are we going to do with them? I'm supposing the thing that follows them is still lurking somewhere."

"You raise a good point, Lottie. I think the best thing at the moment is to put them back where they came from." He pulled the battered wooden container from beneath his counter. "This is what the old bookseller brought them in." They attempted to ring up Mr. Angell, but Charles was surprised to get a disconnect notice from the switchboard operator. "Hmmm, that *is* strange. I wonder what the problem could be."

"Let's go see," offered Theo. Another surprise, appreciating the animosity he had felt toward his competition. Actually, Theo was still experiencing a great sense of adventure and would like to have bragged about it to another interested party. Greta volunteered to watch the bookshop while the other three went. "I hope nothing is wrong," she said, waving them off.

Little was discussed en route to T. T. Angell's home. Charles felt the elation of having all the Bibles safe again, but a sadness had edged its way into his mind. Something deep inside told him that William would never read, and so the wonderful experiences they had all had would never come to the banker. The uneasy feeling that the books must move on to help others also overshadowed him. He would be reluctant to part with the remarkable scriptures and the amazing dreams that had brought them so close together, and so close to the spirit.

A sign was posted on Mr. Angell's mortuary door. It read, *Mortuary Closed—Out of Business. For Excellent Service, Go to Atwood's Mortuary.* A chalky wind swirled around their feet and into their eyes. The door was ajar and swung open in the November breeze. The foyer was empty, swept clean of furniture, flowers, everything.

"Well, I'll be slapped!" declared Theo.

"Good night. He's gone," whispered Lottie.

Charles stood in silence. The memory of the mortician's

face surfaced, and in it he saw the old bookseller once more. "It looks like they all come and go with the wind," he said, speaking mostly to himself.

CHAPTER 35

Good-bye, William

A T THE END of the workday, and after the clerks and officers had left the bank, William Hicken was still clois-
tered in his inner sanctum. Having known nothing about the
break-in, he did not worry over the Bibles. His one regret
was that, in spite of having tried all day to reach Angell, he
would not have the sixth Bible to sell to the mysterious buyer.
When William was flustered, his penchant for detail lost some
of its starch. So it was that when the hour came to trade books
for money, he merely picked up the box and made no detailed
examination. To him, one old Bible was just like another, and
the fact that someone attached great worth to any of them
was an amazement. Obviously, that had not deterred him
from enriching himself.

At the bookstore, the readers had gathered while Theo
and Lottie recounted their story to Dory and Nancy. There
was much laughter and not a little rejoicing. Soon, the evening
dusk began to envelop their small town, and there was talk

of dispersing. Charles switched off the lights, and it became dark inside. Suddenly, they heard the brass bells above the shop entry vibrate energetically. They looked toward the door but saw no one. The bells continued to shake, calling insistently to them. They moved nearer the front of the shop and saw a misty, gray-cloaked figure lingering outside. It was the cricket-man. He seemed agitated, confused and unsteady, like a man on a tight wire. He paced a few moments on the sidewalk and then skirted the square, moving in the direction of the bank.

"Has anybody got a flashlight?" asked Lottie. "That's the man or thing that tried to get my Bible. I think we should follow him."

"Maybe he's the one buying the Bibles from William!" Nancy added.

"Of course! This thing is acting on his own! He has to be the one wanting the books. He really must have made Bill a tremendous offer." Charles yanked the door open and headed into the street. The others followed close by.

The tenuous cricket-man was indeed confused. William had promised that the Bibles were with him; indeed, the shade himself had sensed them behind the walls of the bank. However, passing the bookstore just now, the insect-man had the distinct impression that the Bibles were inside. Their presence always pulled at him, drawing him with a magnetic force and taunting him. He continued his unsure journey now to the bank. Upon arrival, he discovered William standing just outside, bearing a small box. The cricket-man reached into his cloak and withdrew a packet of bills, large denominations every one.

"Are we in accord then?" he asked of the banker. "Do you have them all this time?"

"No. The mortician, Angell, has apparently left town and taken his with him. Five is what I have, but five that otherwise might still be floating around out there. Pay me the money, and they are all yours." Bill was sorry about the sixth

Bible but assured himself of a substantial reward nonetheless. He extended the box toward the cricket-man. In turn, the transparent figure handed him the packet. It took most of the shade's strength to hold up the box, but he was managing well.

William stuffed the money into his overcoat pocket and mumbled a word or two of it having been "nice to deal with you." The sentiment was not returned, but the man wheeled about on insect legs and started in the direction of the cemetery. He had not taken more than a few steps when a grotesque shriek erupted from his already disintegrating throat. "Fool!" he screamed. "They have tricked you! *These are not the right Bibles!*"

William watched as the man dropped the box and came at him, flailing his stick arms and legs in the murky dusk. William was suddenly frightened and again saw before him the pulsating mass that had clawed at his window. He fell backward against the brick wall of the bank building. At once, the group of readers ran to his aid, shining the flashlight in the direction of the retreating heap of cloud and shouting. Charles retrieved the spilled contents of the box and carried it back to the bank, where the group clustered anxiously around Bill Hicken.

"He must have knocked his head against the wall," said Lottie. "He's out like a light."

"We'd better call a doctor or something." Nancy cradled Bill's head in her lap, concerned about his state.

"I think perhaps it is too late for a doctor." A barely audible, raspy whisper penetrated the bustle of the readers' company. Charles looked up to see the old seller of books standing just beyond the huddled group.

"Look at him, Theo. See if I'm not right."

Charles rose to get a clearer view of the old man.

"Yes, Charles. It is I. I've come to take the books back."

Theo sucked in a grating breath and declared loudly, "By jingoes, he's right! Bill is gone!"

"Look in his pocket. Tell me what you see." The old

bookseller pointed to William's lifeless body.

"That's where he put the money," said Greta. "I wouldn't touch it."

"Go ahead, Charles. You do it." The old man spoke quietly and forcefully. Charles obeyed him immediately. He gingerly lifted the lifeless arm and reached into the coat pocket. His hand moved gently in its confines but could locate no money. Instead, when he pulled out his hand, the fingers were coated with a fine dust.

"Poor Bill," whispered the ancient bookseller. "Even if he were alive, that's all he would have to show for his effort."

Dory and Nancy reached for each other and clung together, afraid. Lottie's flashlight was still trained on the dead William Hicken. Theo stood up, shaking his head and clicking his tongue, wishing he had a cigar in his mouth at the moment. Charles put his arm around Greta and held her close. There were a few seconds of silence.

"Well, Charles?" said the bookseller. "Was I not right about the Bibles? Were they not worth much more than you paid for them?"

"They were of infinite worth," Charles replied. "Everyone here discovered that, except for Bill. I don't know what to say. They will be hard to give up."

He looked around his little flock. All of them understood who the weathered old man really was. The women's eyes were filled with tears. Theo looked uncomfortably emotional. He himself felt a hot jab at his throat. Suddenly, Dory uttered at plea. "Please, sir. Couldn't we just read one more story? One more parable together? Something we'd never forget?"

"One more?" The seller of books rearranged his tatters and peered from one reader to another. In their eyes he read the same plea. "Well, just one then. But tomorrow I must be on my way. There are people elsewhere who need messages as badly as you did." So saying, he shuffled away, leaving them to take care of the business of Bill, and the business of dreaming.

CHAPTER 36

The Last Dream

AFTER THE SHERIFF had made his notes and filled out his forms, the group was dismissed. The final analysis was that Bill had suffered a heart attack and fallen against the building. His family was notified, and Mrs. Hicken spoke with Theo about arrangements. He assured her that Bill was in a better place now. *Well, a different place, anyway,* he thought to himself.

They returned to the bookshop and took the Bibles from the worn box. As they pondered which story ought to be read, the readers found themselves gravitating, each one, toward the second chapter of St. Luke, verses one through twenty, the glorious account of the Nativity. That night, the readers began their journey on a crowded highway leading from the city of Nazareth in Galilee to the small town of Bethlehem in Judea. As common folk, they traveled many days to cover the distance of sixty-five miles. They were all there, side by side, journeying to pay tribute money to Caesar Augustus. It seems our travelers knew each other well and had decided to make the pilgrimage together.

Their road cut through dewy waysides, and the sunsets that fell on them were as ripe in color as summer peaches. They awoke to the pearled pink of dawn each day, gathered their belongings, and moved on. Gentle hillocks beckoned them from the distance, and bright stars winked at them when night fell. The usual annoyances met them on the road as well. The crowds stirred dust on every side, dust that filled their noses and mouths. Animals trod deliberately ahead and behind, bellowing or braying in their ears. Bothersome pebbles worked into their pliant leather sandals, and nomadic winds blew against their faces. Except for Theo Atwood, our pilgrims had worn these clothes before. Their long robes gathered the dirt of the road; their hems were worn and soiled from much use. They all walked along the way, even the young girl, Dory, and each carried a flask of animal skin for water. In all, however, the journey was pleasant, since they enjoyed one another's company.

It happened that as they approached the outskirts of Bethlehem, they came upon a man and his wife, who was about to deliver a child. She was young, not unlike Dory, and burdened the small donkey she rode with her weight. The couple traveled slower than most and often were rudely brushed by the crowds. Nancy, the one woman in the group who had borne children, looked on the woman with special sympathy. The streets were so crowded that they remained in close proximity to the couple. Time and again, the readers heard the same response, "I have no more rooms," or "not in your condition. Move on."

Nancy could see that the new mother's time was near, and she stayed within earshot. Fate delivered them all to the same road to find rest. Lottie, Greta, Nancy, and Dory pitched a small camp in the street near a stable where the woman and man had been offered sweet straw for their beds. Well, it was better than nothing, they all reasoned, and settled in to sleep.

Charles and Theo decided to pitch a tent in an open field nearby and sleep under the sky's expanse. Sometime during the night, the women were awakened by their fellow travelers' eager voices. "Come, see in the field. It is unbelievable!"

Together they fled the streets of Bethlehem and rushed to the field. Their way was lit by a magnificent resplendent beam that seemed to bloom and burst like a new planet in the sky. It was a star, lighting all of the sleeping Bethlehem in the middle of the night. Theo and Charles led the others to a small rise at the edge of the field.

There was no need to point to the source of their amazement. They looked down on a small group of shepherds. They could see that the shepherds were gazing to the sky, excited and virtually overcome with awe. Music came from a distance, such melody as they had never heard before. Their ears strained to hear more, and, within a short time, the music gained strength. Brightness filled the vault above the shepherds. Suddenly, the music took a clearer form. They heard voices coming from the night sky and saw the heavenly host spoken of in the account, praising God. "Glory to God in the highest," the travelers heard, "And on earth, peace, good will toward men."

The display continued for a few brilliant minutes, and then the angels were removed again to heaven. The shepherds deliberated among themselves and turned toward Bethlehem. The little group of observers knew at once that they would follow. To their surprise, the shepherds, guided by the brightest of stars, ended the pursuit at the stable near their small camp. The shepherds approached the manger, reverently and almost gingerly. The readers watched from behind, sharing in the wonder. One of the shepherd boys neared the sleeping baby and reached out to touch his tender face. The baby's mother did not restrain him. Instead, she smiled compassionately and allowed him to touch the child.

"What is the holy baby's name?" he asked.

"He is to be called Jesus of Nazareth," the woman answered quietly. "The firstborn son."

The only sounds heard after that were the gentle lowing of the cow in the stable and the cooing of a night bird somewhere in the rafters. Strangely, then, the scene began to dissolve before the readers. Sleep overcame each one, and they remembered nothing until morning. "Jesus of Nazareth," Theo murmured upon awakening. "The firstborn son," whispered Nancy. And so it went, each one repeating the mother's words. They had dreamed their last dream and walked in holy places for the last time.

CHAPTER 37

The Question of Angels

I T WAS ONE of those mornings that occasionally interrupts the chill of autumn in that brief interval so commonly called Indian summer around those parts. The sun was rising warm and golden, filtered by morning mist against a crystal blue expanse. Charles was the first to awake. The finespun dawn was a fitting compliment to the shared dream. His dream, indeed all of the dreamer's images of the night before, had been a spiritual experience, strong enough to carry each of them through many a future storm. This pristine morning pronounced a type of otherworldly "Amen" on the events of the night before.

The seller of books was waiting by the door when Charles arrived to open his shop. The old man looked beggarly standing there in his ragged coat and bent hat. A passerby might have offered him a coin or two if the hat had been in his hand. His expression was one of kindly apology. Charles nodded to him and unlocked the door.

The bells jingled once more as they entered. Charles went to the counter and removed the weathered box from its place below. He opened it carefully to have one last look at the Bibles. The old seller of books waited patiently while Charles gently separated one and leafed through the frail pages. At last, he replaced the Bible, sliding the smooth wood lid of the box shut. He held it up for a moment. Finally, Charles turned the box over to the old man. The bookseller received it reverently and then brushed across the floor to leave. "Good-bye, Charles. I thank you and all of the others for returning the books in perfect order. They are beautiful, are they not?"

"They are the most beautiful books I have ever seen," answered Charles. "Where will you go now?"

"I hear there are souls over in Clairesville in need of these Bibles. I believe that's where I'll go next."

Charles did dare to ask one more question. "What about the dark shadow that follows you, that follows the Bibles? Does he haunt you everywhere you go?"

"Oh, he's all over the place, Charles, don't you know that? He just has to manifest himself more strongly where these special Bibles are. It's because of their power, you see. I dare say that you could spy his influence around just about any day, if you knew what to look for."

"I'm sure that at least six of us here know what to look for now." After a slight hesitation, Charles continued, "I want to thank you. And I want to thank Mr. Angell. I understand he's gone over to Clairesville himself. If you see him, say hello and give him my thanks as well."

"If I see him," chuckled the old bookseller, "I will surely do that. Good-bye now, Charles." He flashed Charles a smile, revealing a familiar gold tooth. Then he opened the door and was gone.

Charles closed the door gently, placing his hand against the window, feeling the warmth of the morning sun. In a few moments, the brass bells were silent and the bookshop was empty, but Charles did not feel alone.

Some say angels have wings and halos. Some say they play harps and guard us from above. As Charles went back to his everyday work, he pondered the question of angels. Perhaps angel wings and halos and harps really did exist, or perhaps they were only lovely props for paintings and hymns. However, in Charles's mind, angels would ever after be dressed in tatters and dust; they would always be soft spoken, gentle but firm. He would forever think of angels skittering like leaves across his shop floor or following an autumn country road on the way to Clairesville.

About the Author

O N THE LIVING room floor of an Ohio walkup apartment some years ago, Barbara came forth a squalling new infant on the pages of the Halloween edition of the *Columbus Dispatch*. For lack of a crib, she spent some baby time in an empty dresser drawer. These events no doubt account for her interest in the written word and a slight case of claustrophobia. While growing up in the Midwest drawing in the margins of her ChildCraft books and composing less than free verse, Barbara learned early that a good sense of humor will see you a long way through life.

Barbara has been an illustrator and editor and a participant in many humanitarian efforts, often using her ability to defend herself in Spanish.

After forty years of marriage, child rearing, and doggedly pursuing these artistic interests, she acknowledges her family as her greatest love, her faith as her greatest anchor, and her husband, Ron, as her best friend. As a woman of a certain age, Barbara also gives credit to her hair stylist, Roberta North (who is *not* like Lottie Mariah); her dentist, Dr. Mike VanLeeuwen; and her orthopedic surgeon, Dr. Kim Bertin. Without these people she would not be the woman she is today.